FATE OF OUR FUTURE

BRIANN DANAE

MESSAGE

Gentle reminder... just because *you* wouldn't doesn't mean someone else can't. Also, this is fiction. Enjoy, and happy reading!

CONVENIENCE
DESTINY
HONOR
TRUST
DEVOTION

CONTENTS

PLAYLIST

If you're a music lover like me, enjoy the playlist I created to feel all the vibes while reading or after you're done. Tap the link, add it to your library, and enjoy!

Apple Music

Spotify Music

PROLOGUE

"YOU GOTTA TELL ME SOMETHING MORE THAN THAT."

PROLOGUE

The Past

Amira perched on the edge of her seat, her fingers drumming lightly against her notebook. Most days, she was prepared for class to end. Today, Professor Ross had captured her attention. Her smooth and deliberate voice filled the lecture hall as she paced in front of the whiteboard.

"Fate," she said, underlining the word with an orange marker. "It's a concept that has captivated humanity for centuries. The idea that our lives are predestined and shaped by forces beyond our control. But what does fate *really* mean?"

Amira stifled a sigh and forbade herself from raising her hand. In theory, she loved philosophical discussions, but in practice—especially during a class that was supposed to end in less than five minutes—she couldn't get wrapped up in her outlook. The class would definitely go over.

Professor Ross turned, her sharp gaze sweeping the room. "So, tell me. Is fate an immutable force, or is it simply a story we tell ourselves to make sense of chaos?"

The room was silent, except for the occasional clearing of throats and shuffling of bodies in seats. Amira fixed her eyes on her notebook, reading the day's date before sketching clouds around it. She wasn't in the mood to play philosopher today.

"Miss Scott," Professor Ross said, her voice slicing through the silence.

Amira's pen froze mid-doodle. She sat up straighter, with a neutral expression, and sighed.

"Yes?"

"What is your outlook on fate?" Professor Ross questioned.

Of course, she'd ask me, Amira thought, but gladly answered.

"I think it depends on perspective," she began cautiously. "For some, fate is comforting...an explanation for why things happen. For others, it's a way to avoid accountability. But maybe fate isn't absolute. Maybe it's just potential, shaped by our choices."

Professor Ross tilted her head, considering her words. "Interesting. Potential rather than certainty. A blend of agency and inevitability. And how do you think literature reflects that?"

Amira hesitated, her mind scrambling for a relevant example. She was used to being put on the spot.

"I think it's in how characters often wrestle with whether they're in control or being controlled," she answered.

Professor Ross tilted her head, urging her to continue with her explanation.

"Take *Oedipus Rex,* for example," Amira continued. "He tries to defy the prophecy, but every choice he makes brings him closer to fulfilling it. Is that considered fate, or just a series of decisions driven by his fear of it?"

Professor Ross nodded, a glimmer of enthusiasm in her demeanor. "That's an excellent observation, Ms. Scott. The intersection of choice and destiny is at the heart of so many great stories. I hope everyone was listening."

Amira smiled. She made her point sound effortless, which was a struggle for most students. Professor Ross wrapped up the lecture, reminding them about their upcoming essay on fate in litera-ture. Amira shoved her notebook and folder inside her backpack and slid her arms through the straps before filing up the stairs. She was almost out of the side door when a familiar voice called out for her to slow down.

"Aye, Amira! Hold up."

She paused and sighed inwardly, wondering what he wanted today. After every class, Brent found something to spark up a conversation with her about. He maneuvered through the students with an urgency that almost made Amira chuckle. He approached her with his locs swinging and a smile that made her shake her head.

"What you shaking your head for?" Brent asked.

"Because... what can I help you with today? It's always something."

He chuckled, watching her shift her weight from one foot to the other. Amira did nothing to hide her impatience.

"You saying it like I get on your nerves."

Amira tilted her head with raised brows, hoping he caught the hint. "You're almost there."

"A'ight, a'ight," he said with a smirk, unfazed by her clipped tone. "I was trying to invite you to me and my brothers' party this weekend."

Her eyes drifted to the gold and black shirt with 1906 below bold letters. Brent and his boys were known to throw the best parties. It was how Amira met him last year. Attending a PrettyNasty party as a freshman blew her mind, and she wanted no part of the festivities this weekend.

"Thank you, but I'll pass. I have a lot of work to catch up on," Amira said, angling her body to walk off.

It wasn't a complete lie but not the entire truth. Brent didn't need to know that.

"One night of kicking it ain't gon' set you back," Brent replied. "Lowkey, I think you trying to avoid me."

Amira's laugh was short and humorless. "If I wanted to avoid you, I would've kept on walking."

Smirking, he adjusted his backpack. "Fair point. You must have a man, then."

"I do," Amira said proudly. Boldly.

She was being polite, but Brent needed to know that whatever he was trying to pursue with her would never come to fruition. He looked almost surprised but still determined.

"Word? He go here?"

Amira shook her head. "No. But that doesn't matter. You and I will never be a thing." She smiled and patted his arm before walking off. "Have a good day!"

Brent stood there for a moment, watching her stride down the sidewalk with a mean ass walk, and mumbled, "Yeah... you, too."

A small smile tugged at Amira's lips as she walked to her dorm. Brent wasn't the first guy who tried pushing up on her since she started Southern State, and he wouldn't be the last, but she was in a committed relationship. One that had her rushing to her dorm room to study and clean up so she could talk to Saleem when he called.

Amira waved at a girl down the hall before entering the suite she shared with three other girls. The fresh scent of peaches from the plug-ins she bought the day before wafted through her nose and continued to linger as she walked into her room. Thankfully, her roommate and friend, Jazmine, wasn't here yet. Amira wanted to study in peace and possibly get a nap in. According to the time on her phone, she had a good two hours to do just that before Saleem called or Jazmine returned.

Minutes floated by, and before she knew it, the timer she set went off, startling her from the slow nod she almost gave into. Amira shut her MacBook with a sigh and pushed her books to the side of her brown desk that doubled as a vanity. Tapping the screen of her phone that laid beside an empty mug once filled with coffee, she frowned.

No missed calls from Saleem.

There were no texts either.

Her thumb hovered over his name in her call log. Before calling, she replayed their conversation from earlier in the day in her mind, searching for a trace of miscommunication.

"Baby, I'ma call you before I meet with a few class-mates," Saleem said.

"And what time is that?"

He paused for a few seconds. "About five forty-five."

"Okay."

Her reply was clear and straightforward, and so was his time. Five forty-five had passed twenty-two minutes ago. She tapped his name before her over-thinking could get the best of her. Surely, something had come up. The phone didn't ring once before his voicemail picked up. She only caught his smooth baritone announcing his name before hanging. Dialing him back, figuring it was a mishap, she was greeted with the same results.

"You've reached Saleem. Leave a message and—"

Amira jammed her thumb into the screen, ending the call. She wished she still had her pink

Razr phone to flip it closed, displaying her now foul mood. Before her attitude had time to settle, worry took its place. Saleem was in his first year of graduate school, so something might have come up.

This wasn't like him.

He was dependable. Saleem stuck to his word if he said he would do something, and Amira hated how quickly she thought of the worst happening. It wasn't fair to him or her, but they'd made an agreement when they decided to be in a long-distance relationship.

"Never have me wondering what's going on with you," Amira said. "I don't like worrying."

Saleem kissed her lips that were poked out as she pouted. "I won't. I promise."

Again, her words were clear, and so was his reply. Yet, Amira was feeling the effects of his broken promise. Doubt slithered into her chest like an unwelcome guest, aching her heart. A question that had been lingering in her mind for weeks resurfaced, and she shook her head to clear it.

"No. It wasn't foolish to agree to be in a long-distance relationship. He'll call back." She huffed and stood from her desk.

Needing something to lift her dampened mood, Amira dragged her feet toward the mini fridge on the opposite side of their room. She had her mind set on the mini strawberry cheesecake bites, but when she opened the door, she was greeted with nothing.

"Are you serious!" she semi-shouted just as their main dorm room opened.

Jazmine entered their bedroom with a confused expression. "What's the matter?"

"Jaz, I know you didn't eat my damn cheesecake bites. I told you to grab your own when we were at the store, and you swore you didn't want any. So, why are mine missing?"

Amira's chest heaved as she went off. One too many times, Jazmine had *accidentally* eaten her snacks. Her weed-induced munchies always got the best of her. Amira would let it slide any other day, but after her unanswered calls to Saleem, she had to say something.

"Well, hello to you too, Ms. Grumpy." Jazmine chuckled. "If you must know... I did eat them last night while you were snoring."

"I don't snore!" Amira snapped.

"Sometimes." Jazmine smirked. "But I replaced them."

She held up a bag from the local grocery store. Inside were the cheesecake bites and some other goodies she had to have when it was that time of the month. They'd been roommates since freshman year and didn't mind sharing things, just as long as they were replaced and knew what was off-limits.

"Here," Jazmine said, handing them to her. "I know you aren't in a shitty mood all because of these."

Amira rolled her eyes as Jazmine unbagged her things. Her long box braids swung as she maneuvered around her side of the room. Her mocha brown complexion looked radiant in the mustard-colored track suit she wore.

"Thank you, and no. Saleem isn't answering the phone."

"Oh, goodness. He does have a life outside of y'all's relationship," Jazmine said, putting her shoes on the rack at the end of her bed.

Amira sucked her teeth. "Obviously, but that's not the point. Maybe he should just have a life without me in it."

Jazmine turned around so quickly, she bumped her knee on the edge of her bed. "Dammit!" She hissed, rubbing what she knew would later be a bruise. "Mira... please. You're overreacting."

"Am I, though? You'd be thinking the same thing

if your man's phone went to voicemail after he said he'd call you at a specific time and didn't."

Jazmine hummed and tilted her head. "I mean…"

"Exactly. I'm too young to be stressing over a man and these classes. It only makes sense to be single. Plus, I feel like I'm not getting the full college experience."

Squinting, Jazmine shook her head. "So, that's what it is? You feel like you're missing out?"

"Sometimes." Amira shrugged.

She hadn't always felt like this, but something in her gut was telling her to end things before she got her heart broken.

"Trust me, you're not. Saleem is so good to you. You can't convince me that him not answering your calls led to you wanting to break up. I'm not buying that mess, girl." Jazmine chuckled, waving her off. "Plus, what do you want to do while you're single that you can't do in a relationship?"

"I don't know, enjoy the parties more. Not feel guilty about hanging with other dudes when we do go out. Hell, even just having male friends," Amira said and continued. "One missed call or argument between us throws my entire day off, and I don't like that."

"Y'all don't even argue," Jazmine said.

"You don't know what we do. Just because you don't hear it doesn't mean it doesn't happen."

Jazmine lifted her hands. "True. My bad. All couples have disagreements, but I get it. If you don't want to be tied down so you can enjoy your college years, then don't be. Buuut, don't hurt yourself and him in the process. It'd be different if he were out here cheating on you or something."

To Jazmine and Amira's knowledge, Saleem wasn't cheating; never had and never would cheat on her. The thought that it could happen made Amira's stomach toil with unease. She didn't want to hurt him just as much as she didn't want to hurt herself.

"Yeah," Amira mumbled, sitting in her chair. "Maybe I'm tripping."

"A little, but your feelings are valid. Just tell him how you feel when he calls back," Jazmine suggested.

Amira planned to do just that. When her phone vibrated against the desk with an incoming call, she flinched and eagerly grabbed it. She immediately got annoyed when she realized it wasn't Saleem but one of the girls she met and worked with through her work-study job at the psychology department.

"That's not him?" Jazmine asked.

"No," Amira huffed, and her brows dipped,

seeing Jazmine grab her shower caddy. "Where you about to go?"

"My lil' friends' house. You wanna come with me?"

Jazmine had a few *lil' friends*, and Amira hoped she wasn't having sex with all of them. But, if she was, that was her prerogative. She didn't judge her and always prayed that she was safe.

"Which lil' friend? Because the last house we went over to, they were trying to teach me how to hit a bong." Amira scrunched her face up. "That's too crack-headish for me."

Jazmine busted out laughing. "Girl, shut up! No, it isn't. That's regular for some smokers. Everyone thinks you're this hippie-ass chick because of all your tattoos and that one loc in your head."

Her dark brown hair with a honey-blonde streak was pulled into a messy bun while that singular loc hung loosely down her back. Amira tried something different with her hair last year and kept one of her two-strand twists in to see what would happen. After some months, the hair loc'd, and she loved it, so she kept it.

She had a sleeve full of colorful tattoos that popped gorgeously against her honey brown skin. She'd gotten them throughout high school and even some in the last few years. The right side of her back, up to her shoulder, was etched with a horizontal view of the night sky, clouds, and stars. Subtle lines connected to form constellations, while the rest of her body was marked with small, meaningful ink. Stereotyping her just because she loved getting tattoos and had a unique hairstyle was wild to Amira, but what else was new for a Black woman?

"You know I don't care what people think. I don't even like people for real," Amira stated.

Chuckling, Jazmine said, "Right. Very nice, not so friendly. How did we become friends again?"

"You wouldn't leave me alone, and I had to be cordial since we shared a room," Amira said, trying not to grin.

"Oh, girl, please." Jazmine laughed. "Like I was pressed to be friends with you. You wouldn't have survived freshman year without me."

"*We* wouldn't have survived it without each other," Amira clarified.

"Touché. I'm going to shower. Don't be single when I get out."

Amira rolled her eyes as Jazmine walked out of the room. She wouldn't make any promises. Instead of focusing on the negative, she popped the lid on her cheesecake bites and indulged. The silence in the room irked her nerves to no end, forcing her mind to wander right back to why she was scarfing down the sweet dessert as if it were her last.

Saleem must've felt her doubts growing because the next time her phone vibrated, it was an incoming call from him. Amira quickly swallowed what she was chewing and cleared her throat.

"Hello," she answered, trying to sound as casual as possible.

"Baby, what's up? Damn, I missed you all day," he said, voice soothing and warm but rushed. "I meant to call you earlier, but my phone died on my way to the library."

"Oh. Okay," Amira murmured. "I missed you, too. You had me thinking something was wrong, and then—"

She stopped talking when she heard a girl's voice much too close to the speaker.

"Finally, found a charger, huh?" the girl asked.

Saleem chuckled, and Amira's stomach churned.

"Yeah, 'preciate you."

"No problem. Are you coming with us to get some food?"

Amira exhaled so harshly that you'd think she was out of breath.

"Hello!" she shouted, catching herself and Saleem off guard.

The girl, too, because her eyes widened. He didn't have Amira on speaker; that's just how loud she was. Saleem shook his head, no, and she exited the study lounge.

"What you doing all that hollering for?" Saleem asked.

"Because... am I interrupting something? Let me know," Amira spat, unable to keep her tone neutral.

"Interrupting? Nah. That's just Brandi, one of the girls from the group. We were wrapping everything up," Saleem explained casually.

Amira clenched her jaw. She'd heard him mention Brandi before. "And you were using her charger?"

"Yes, baby. I left mine in the car rushing in here, and I just went to grab it. What's the matter? You sound all hostile like you need to get something off your chest." He chuckled, not realizing the severity of his words or the moment.

Drawing in a stuttered breath, Amira closed her eyes. "I don't think we should be together anymore."

Saleem stopped gathering the papers scattered across the table.

"What did you just say?" His voice was sharp,

laced with confusion. Her words had caught him completely off guard.

Amira's chest tightened before saying, "This long-distance thing... I. I can't do it anymore."

Her throat burned as the words tumbled out of her mouth. They sounded foreign to her, so she knew Saleem was having difficulty comprehending them.

"Amira," he said cautiously. "Angel Face," he said, calling her by the nickname assigned by him.

She had the meanest mug when he approached her in the store when they first met. Then, Saleem made her smile by simply asking how her day was going. The mug dropped, and her serene aura blanketed him. Being in her presence felt otherworldly, and she became his angel, but he couldn't help but feel like she was being everything but one right now. Amira's eyes watered, and she squeezed them shut. He was breaking her resolve by calling her that. She shook her head, quietly telling him no, and he felt it though he couldn't see her.

"Nah, don't do that. Don't go quiet on me. Qu'est-ce que vous dites en ce moment?"

Amira knew that when he started speaking French, he was extremely serious, pissed, or confused. Right now, he was all three. He could speak many languages, including Darija—his native language—and English. Amira was still learning to understand Darija, which is Moroccan Arabic, so he spoke in French. A common language they both studied and understood. He asked her what she was saying right now as if her words didn't make sense. They didn't.

Amira sniffled, and her voice trembled. "I think it's best that we break up. We're living two different worlds right now, and I just want you to live your best life without worrying about me."

"Amira," he said her name again and chuckled in disbelief. "What the hell do you mean you want me to live my best life without worrying about you? Does that even sound like something I want to do? Did I ask you for that?"

She brushed the tears from her face and shook her head. "No, but—"

"But nothing. You got me real confused right now, baby. For real. Did I do something wrong?"

His voice went softer but still stern and coated her ears like warm honey being poured over her senses. Saleem hadn't done anything wrong, but Amira didn't know how to explain that she felt it in her heart that he would. Or that being away from him for months at a time no longer worked for her.

Or that she knew how he'd only told Brandi no about grabbing something to eat so he could talk to her for the rest of the night.

"No," she choked out. Her chest hiccupped, forcing the word out. "You didn't do anything wrong."

"You gotta tell me something more than that," Saleem pleaded.

Even though the air was on full blast inside the study lounge, the beating of his heart and the warmth of his skin made Saleem feel like he was about to pass out. When she sniffled again, Saleem groaned and ran a hand down his face.

"I don't know. I just feel like you're meeting people, advancing in your field, living your life. I don't want our relationship to hold you back," she said, swallowing hard.

"Hold me back?" His voice inched an octave higher. "It hasn't been stopping anything, so where is this coming from? Are you pregnant and scared?"

Her eyes widened. "What? No! Oh, my gosh, no."

Saleem would've been better off hearing her say yes. At least then, that'd explain why she was ending things between them.

"So, you want to break up because what, again?" He needed her to break this shit down thoroughly.

"I just... I feel like I need to figure out who I am, too. We're young, Saleem. Maybe we should explore more... grow separately."

"Explore what after three years? Ain't shit out there for me but you."

Her chest ached as his tender words washed over her. "I don't want you to wake up one day and regret spending all your time worrying about me, about us, when you could've been living."

Saleem remained silent for a long moment, letting her words marinate. Yes, they made sense, but why now? It wasn't about the unanswered calls and Brandi. Amira had been thinking about this for weeks. When he finally spoke, Saleem's voice was raw and emotional but steady.

"Amira, you don't get to decide that for me. You want a nigga to just stop caring about you, like it's nothing. Like we meant nothing. I don't regret us and never have."

"I just think it's best for right now. Before one of us gets hurt," Amira said.

"This shit is hurting us both right now. You can't see that... can't feel that?"

She did, and pressing her palm against her heart wasn't soothing the pain. Saleem wanted to flip the table over; he was so frustrated and hurt. There was no understanding when it came to his heart and Amira.

"I do," Amira blubbered.

"Nah. You don't. You can't, but if this is what you want, I ain't gon' fight you on it. You know I'd give you anything in this fucking world."

The tense hurt in his voice made her tears roll. Amira covered her mouth with the back of her hand to mask her cries. She was so worried about Saleem breaking her heart, when she should've been more concerned about breaking her own. Anything Amira needed and wanted, Saleem provided.

When her mama kicked her off the phone plan a month into her freshman year and said she needed to learn responsibility and get a job so she could pay the bill, Amira panicked. Although she had jobs in high school, maintaining a job and taking college courses was a different playing field. She mentioned her plans to get a job to Saleem, and he added her to his plan and wired her money every month without thought.

On late nights when she needed to study but was too tired, he would turn it into a game. It was nothing for Saleem to ensure she wasn't stressed about anything and could focus solely on her classes. Never once did he think their relationship was the stressor.

"I don't want you to hate me," Amira whispered.

Saleem was feeling a lot of things right now, but hate wasn't one of them.

"I'll never hate you for following your heart. Even though it's leading you the wrong way," Saleem replied almost bitterly.

He didn't know why she was suddenly fearful of them, but he'd never force his hand.

"And I do love you," she rushed out. "But it's just not the right time."

"Yeah," Saleem mumbled, clearing his throat. "I guess not."

Amira didn't expect him to say he loved her, too. She'd heard him say it a thousand times but it wouldn't have hurt. Maybe it'd help soothe her self-inflicted wound.

"I hope you understand," she said, not knowing what else to say.

"Yeah."

That seemed to be the only word Saleem could muster up. Grabbing his things, he walked out of the study room, bypassing students with a blur.

"So, um... I guess I'll see you around," Amira said, hoping she wouldn't.

They were from the same city, but rarely did he come home. Saleem lived in another state.

"Yeah...you take care, Amira."

His words were so final, and the disconnection of the call made what she'd just done settle in. Sliding the phone onto her desk, Amira stared at it like it was the one in the wrong. Standing up, she blinked through blurry vision while stripping from her clothes. All she wanted to do was climb in bed and cry. The weight of her decision had her curled up in a ball with the covers pulled over her head.

"Mira," Jazmine said, entering the room. She heard sniffling, and she rushed to her side. "Awww, friend. It's gonna be okay. You did what was best." She rubbed her back, and that only made Amira cry harder.

She wanted to believe that she'd done what was best for her... best for them, but her heart felt differently. Jazmine sat with her until her sniffles quieted. Amira laid in silence, listening to her get dressed and mumbled an *mhm* when Jazmine told her she'd be back later. Thoughts of them evaded her mind as sleep took over.

When she finally woke up from what she thought was a bad dream, it was from her body being shaken awake. Disoriented, she heard her other roommate, Whitney, call her name.

"Amira. Wake up."

Blinking through her haze, she wiped her eyes. "What's going on?" she mumbled, yawning.

She didn't know how long she'd slept, but it felt like forever. The dryness of her tears clung to her skin as she wiped at her face.

"Your boyfriend is knocking on the door. We're going to get in trouble if Sarah sees him here," Whitney said.

Their RA, Sarah, was quick to write someone up, especially if it was past curfew. Although they were a co-ed dorm, they had rules to follow. Still, Amira was confused by what she'd just said.

"My boyfriend?"

"Um, yes. You do remember that you have one of those, right?" She chuckled, not knowing Amira was actually single as of five hours ago.

Amira's heart lurched. "What?"

Her eyes shot to her phone, still lying face up on the desk. In haste, she tossed the covers from her body and grabbed it. There were a few missed calls and texts but none from Saleem.

"Um, should I tell him to leave? He's still knocking."

Whitney's question made her tune into the thunderous knocks at their main door. Her mouth fell open after hearing Saleem's voice.

"I ain't leaving until you talk to me, so open the door, baby."

"Oh, my gosh," Amira whispered. "What the hell?"

On autopilot, she rushed to the pile of clothes that needed to be folded at the end of her bed. She tugged a wrinkled SSU shirt over her head and slipped on a pair of shorts. Ironically, the gray basketball shorts belonged to Saleem. She didn't have time to change, though. Nor did she care about her appearance. He wasn't here for the pleasantries, and she knew it.

Rushing into the living area, Amira unlocked and swung the door open before he could knock again and have security come to see what all the noise was about. Saleem's tall, six-foot-three frame filled the doorway, holding a duffle bag in his hand. She pulled him into the room, and her eyes struggled to focus on his face.

Saleem was still wearing his work clothes from earlier in the day: slacks and a white button-down shirt. He didn't have time to change before studying and didn't think about it before driving four hours to see Amira.

She didn't want to stare but couldn't help it. Saleem's warm, golden-brown complexion, neat, straight-back silky braids, and determined copper-hued eyes under the dim lighting made her weak. The shadows underneath his eyes told her he was beyond tired, but sleep could wait.

"Saleem," Amira said slowly, voice just above a whisper.

He looked her dead in the face. Eyes swirling with a mixture of intense hurt and frustration, yet a softness that she pulled out of him without a struggle. That was love lingering—his vulnerability on display in 4K.

"Tell me, Angel. I need to hear you tell me to my face that we're through."

Amira blinked, not believing this was happening. "You... I didn't think you'd—"

"Drive down here to see you?" he said, dropping the bag and stepping her way. "Yeah, I did. Because if you gon' break a nigga's heart, do it in my face."

Her throat tightened, and she looked away, tears filling her eyes. "Saleem, please. You didn't have to—"

Gently, he turned her face towards him. "Yes, I

did," he said firmly. "You don't get to call me, tell me you want to end things, and then give me some half-ass excuse about living my life. You are my life."

Amira's eyes burned as he cupped her face with both hands. Her cheeks were stained with fresh tears as she couldn't contain them.

"Talk to me. I'm right here. Get it all off your chest. I'm sorry for whatever confusion and doubt I may have placed in your mind, baby. You gotta believe me," Saleem pleaded, wiping her tears.

Amira almost fell to her knees when he placed slow, soft kisses all over her face.

Her resolve wavered quickly. Having him touch her and speak those words that shook her core was no match for her poor heart.

"You'll want more," she said, her voice cracking.

"I don't want more. I want you."

"But what if you do? What if I'm keeping you from finding it?"

Saleem shook his head. "Baby, you're talking crazy. I never knew you to be a punk. What you scared of?"

"Us," she said, backing up, breaking their connection. "You'll look back years from now and be mad that I tied you down."

"Tied me down?" he asked incredulously. "You

aren't some weights around my neck that I want to remove. Is this about me taking care of you? That's who I am... that's all I know to do."

She knew that. Saleem valued his Moroccan beliefs from his father's bloodline and easily adapted to his African American mother's roots. Naturally, he was a provider and protector, so him popping up shouldn't have been a shock.

"Is it the distance? What is it?" he asked when she remained silent.

"It's everything," Amira cried. "I'm trying to do what's best for both of us."

Saleem let out a disbelieving laugh, running a hand over his braids. He was ready to rip them out; he was so frustrated. "Do you hear yourself? You don't see me standing here like I don't know what I want?"

Amira stood her ground even with a trembling voice and said, "I do, but I want something different."

Her words hung heavily in the air, damn near choking Saleem. His jaw tightened, and his expression crumbled at the weight of her words.

"Something different, like what?" he asked, hinting at what Amira knew was on his mind.

She shook her head quickly. "No, not someone else. I'm looking for *me*, Saleem. I'm scared that if I stay with you, I'll lose myself in us, and I can't do that. I need to figure out who I am on my own."

His shoulders sagged as he exhaled shakily. That wasn't the answer he expected either, but it was better than he thought. He could work with that. Had no choice but to work with that because Amira wasn't budging.

"Angel, you don't have to do that alone. I'm not holding you back. We can grow together. That's what relationships are about."

"But what if we can't?" she countered, her voice raw with arms stretched as if the answers would be placed in her palms. "What if I hold you back, or you hold me back, and we end up hating each other? I can't risk that. Not with you."

Saleem stared at her, trying to make sense of what she was telling him. "So, that's it? You're just... walking away? After everything?"

She wiped at her cheeks, her heart breaking with every word. "I'm trying to do what's right. I don't want to hurt you more later because I was too scared to let go now."

He let out a bitter laugh, shaking his head. "You

think this doesn't hurt now? Amira, you're breaking my fucking heart. You're breaking *us*."

"I know," she whispered, her voice barely audible. "And I'm sorry."

For a moment, he didn't move, his chest rising and falling as he tried to compose himself. Then, slowly, he nodded, though his expression was full of pain. "Okay," he said hoarsely. "If this is what you really want, I'll respect it and leave you alone to... figure out who you are."

She opened her mouth to speak, but he held up a hand.

"Nah. It's good, baby. No need to keep apologizing. You saved your heart to break mine. That takes some real strength right there, baby. You got it."

Saleem chuckled bitterly and grabbed his duffle bag, slinging it over his shoulder. Walking over to where she stood, he kissed her forehead. Amira held her breath and closed her eyes, inhaling his scent for the last time.

"Take care of yourself, Amira. I hope you find whatever you're searching for," he said sincerely before turning and walking out the door.

Amira stared at the door once it closed, and she finally exhaled. Backing up, she fell into the loveseat, wondering if he meant those words. She tried convincing herself that she'd done the right thing, but her heart felt no lighter about her decision. She didn't even feel her heart.

It was shattered.

1

———

"I'M JUST... LIVING, YOU KNOW? EXISTING."

ONE

Present Day

Being a good person wasn't all it was cracked up to be. Amira had come to that conclusion the second her scandalous landlord called himself trying to evict her. Instead of catching an assault charge and going upside his head like she wanted to do, she took the civil route and took him to court. This was not how she wanted to start her week off but here she was.

Amira clasped her hands at the plaintiff's table as her leg bounced. She'd been living in her townhome for over three years, and not once had there been any issues between her and Mr. Fletcher, her land-lord. Rent was paid on time, her yard was main-tained, and she immediately let him know if she had any maintenance issues. Glancing to her left, Amira wondered what the problem was. Seeing the smirk on his face made Amira's stomach churn, and she grit her teeth. She was at risk of being homeless if today didn't go in her favor, and he was amused.

"All rise," the bailiff announced, prompting everyone to stand.

Judge Melissa Saunders, a no-nonsense Black woman with kind eyes and a calm demeanor, sat behind the bench. Her shiny silk press and cour-teous smile didn't prepare Amira for the tongue-lashing she was about to give out.

"You may be seated," Judge Saunders said, scan-ning the courtroom.

Her gaze landed on Amira and then Mr. Fletcher. She read over their file and addressed Amira first.

"Ms. Scott, you're the tenant. Please state your case."

Clearing her throat, Amira stood up. "Good afternoon, Your Honor. I've been living in my town-home for three years. Last month, Mr. Fletcher sent me a text message claiming I had to move out because he was renting the unit to someone else."

"And was your lease up?" Judge Saunders asked.

"No, Your Honor. My lease is still active."

The judge told her to proceed.

"According to my lease, he's required to give me sixty days' notice. And not through a text message," Amira said, trying to keep her tone neutral.

It was so unprofessional, and she hoped nothing good would come to him after this. Amira wasn't the type to pray on someone's downfall, but Mr. Fletcher's karma was going to be nasty. Judge Saunders nodded and turned her attention toward him.

"Mr. Fletcher, is this true?"

"Your Honor, I let Ms. Scott know she had thirty days to vacate, which I believe is more than reasonable. If you ask me, she's been difficult and uncooperative about this transition."

"Uncooperative?" Amira scoffed under her breath and sucked her teeth. "You can't be serious."

Judge Saunders glanced her way. "Ms. Scott, you'll have your turn to speak again." Her voice was firm but not unkind. "Now, Mr. Fletcher, did you comply with the terms of the lease agreement?"

Mr. Fletcher shifted his feet, a sure sign that he was about to make up some bullshit. "Circumstances change. The sixty-day clause is standard, but I needed to make a few arrangements. Ms. Scott—"

"Isn't in violation of anything according to this lease," she said, cutting him off while holding up some papers. "While I understand circumstances change, an agreement is just that. It is unlawful and a shame that you felt it was okay to make this decision and through a text message at that." She shook her head and faced Amira. "Ms. Scott, what relief are you seeking today?"

Amira stood again, taking a deep breath. "I'm not trying to be difficult, and I haven't been since I moved in. This all came out of nowhere, so I need more time to find a new place. Thirty days isn't nearly enough, especially with the way the rental market looks right now. Although I shouldn't be getting put out, to begin with, I'm asking for an additional thirty days to figure some things out. And for Mr. Fletcher to stop harassing me about moving."

Judge Saunders leaned back in her chair. She knew what her decision would be the second she read over the documents. Her expression was unreadable, and Amira hoped today weighed in her favor.

"Mr. Fletcher," she began, "while I understand landlords have the right to manage their properties how they see fit, you are bound by the lease agreement you signed. The sixty-day notice is there for a reason, and you failed to honor it."

The smirk Mr. Fletcher sported since he walked in, vanished.

"Furthermore, harassing anyone, but especially a woman, with hopes to get her out quicker will have you placed in cuffs faster than you can blink."

Mr. Fletcher gulped. He didn't think his text messages throughout the day about him tossing her things out were taken seriously.

"As for you, Ms. Scott," she continued, "you are entitled to the sixty days outlined in your lease. However, since part of that time has already elapsed, I'll grant you an additional thirty days from tomorrow to vacate the premises."

She glanced at her calendar and calculated how many days Amira had to be gone.

"That gives you forty-two days to get your affairs in order. Unfortunately, situations like these do arise unexpectedly. I wish you the best."

Amira exhaled, relief washing over her. "Thank you."

Judge Saunders gave a curt nod. "I advise both parties to use this time wisely. Court is adjourned."

She struck the gravel and stood. Amira gathered her things and avoided Mr. Fletcher's glare as she walked past him. The man had been pissing her off for weeks now and thought he was about to get over on her. It would've been one thing had Amira been a horrible tenant and broken the rules of her lease, but that hadn't been the case.

Amira stepped out of the courtroom into the dimly lit hallway, and her nostrils flared at the sound of Mr. Fletcher calling her name. She didn't know why he suddenly had a change of heart, but she wasn't in the mood to hear why now. It didn't matter that Judge Saunders had given her extra time to move; the fact remained that he was a scandalous landlord.

She wanted to bask in relief, but Amira was angry. An impromptu move just when she'd taken over new cases at work and right before the new year was ridiculous. The thought of searching for a place made her head throb. The number of days she had to get her life together was on rotation in her head as she made it to her car.

"Ugh," she huffed, cranking the heat up after starting it. "I need a drink."

Grabbing her phone out of her purse, Amira went to her text messages. Pulling up the thread between her, Jazmine, Leerah, Sovanna, and her cousin, Quinn, she sent them a message.

Amira: *I'm leaving court and need a drink. Who's off?*

A text from Sovanna immediately came through, and Amira smiled. Even though Sovanna lived in Houston, they never made her feel left out.

Sovanna: *I'm at work all the way in a different state, but I'll have one for you when I get off. How'd it go?*

Jazmine: *I'm taking my hour lunch in a few minutes. Meet me at Juvie's. I need some chicken so bad it's not funny.*

Chuckling, Amira started typing a reply when an incoming call interrupted her. The unsaved number moving across the screen was one she knew by heart now, but she hadn't saved it yet for a reason.

"Hello," Amira answered.

"What's going on? How was court?" Chris, a guy she'd been dating for the last few months, asked.

Amira sighed. "Technically, I won. She granted me an extra thirty days to move out, but I still have to move."

"Damn. That's all bad," Chris said.

"Right. I'm already stressed thinking about all the packing, moving, deposits, and who knows what else. And it's at the worst time of the year."

"He could've at least waited until the new year to

pull this stunt. Don't trip about packing. You got weekends off, so you can knock most of it out then."

His suggestion sounded nice, but Amira still rolled her eyes. Chris hadn't offered one solution or extended a helping hand. It didn't matter that she was off on weekends. Packing up a three-story, four-bedroom townhome by herself wasn't ideal. To see where his mind was at in terms of helping her, Amira kept talking. She didn't expect any handouts, but damn. It was the least he could've offered. Alleviating some of her stress would've been nice, considering they were dating. It was nothing serious and far from a relationship, but still.

"True. I just wish there was more I could do on such short notice." She sighed.

"You'll figure it out. In the meantime, pull up on me. I got something that'll help you ease some of that stress away," Chris teased.

Amira's top lip curled with annoyance, and her nostrils flared with disgust. This was exactly why she hadn't saved his number. *Men are a fucking joke. A damn disgrace,* she thought.

Chuckling, she said, "Pull up on you, huh?"

"Yeah. Why you say it like that?"

"Did you not hear anything I just said?"

There was no way he was on her phone thinking

some dick would erase her problems. She just knew that wasn't the extravagant advice he had.

"Yeah, and I'm telling you to stop worrying about everything. You always figure it out. That's what I like about you," Chris said, making Amira even more annoyed.

I'm tired of having to figure it out, nigga, damn, she thought. For once in her life, Amira didn't want to have to think about anything. She didn't want to have to come up with some elaborate plan to piece her life back together in forty-two freaking days. Nor did she want to *pull up* on a man who could only offer dick during a crisis. It was good dick, but that wasn't the point.

"Yeah, I bet. Look, I'm about to grab some food with my homegirls. I'll call you later," Amira said, pulling out of the parking lot.

"A'ight. Don't forget," Chris said.

"Of course not."

Amira lied straight through her teeth. She was going to do more than forget about calling him back. Going to his number, she added it to the block list. Chris wasn't obligated to do anything for her, and Amira didn't feel compelled to keep in contact with a man who offered the bare minimum. It was a harsh reality on both ends, but it was life. It was handing her a deck of cards she had no choice but to shuffle and choose wisely from. Keeping a man around who wasn't resourceful was a choice Amira wasn't electing.

"I'm about to be homeless, and he's talking about giving me some dick. What I'ma do, find shelter under his balls once I'm evicted?" Amira asked, making Jazmine choke on the fries she just shoved in her mouth.

Quinn cackled loudly before tossing a hand over her mouth. "Mira," she wheezed, reaching for her water.

"What?" Amira asked. "I'm serious."

"That's the problem." Jazmine laughed. "You be so serious, and that's what makes things funnier."

Amira shrugged. She truly wanted to know what was running through Chris' mind earlier. She would never know since his calls and messages couldn't get through. While Leerah declined to meet them, Jazmine and Quinn pulled into the parking lot at the same time. Having just lost her child's father the month prior, Amira knew Leerah more than likely wouldn't come out but she never hesitated to ask. Not including her didn't feel right.

All the women, except Jazmine and Quinn, attended high school together and remained good friends throughout college. Amira didn't consider herself as close as Leerah and Sovanna were, but they were still her girls. Maintaining friendships for almost two decades was tough, but they did it. Amira was so happy when she and Jazmine graduated, and she moved to her hometown for a job she accepted. Her friend group was small, but she loved them regardless.

"Everyone is just taking me for a joke today." Amira pouted.

Quinn shook her head. She knew her cousin better than anyone and wasn't trying to make her feel worse than she already was. "You're the one tossing out jokes. But for real... you know if it comes down to you needing somewhere to stay, my door is always open."

"Mine, too," Jazmine added. "It's not like we haven't lived together before."

They'd never let her be out here seeking shelter, and Amira appreciated them for that. She took a generous swig of her peach margarita.

"Thank y'all. It's all just so annoying," she said.

"You should've smacked him upside his bald head." Jazmine grimaced.

Quinn agreed. "For real, Mira. You're too nice."

"So, y'all wanted me to put my hands on a grown ass man, get taken to jail, and put out of my home?"

"Hell, you would've had a warm place to stay for a while," Jazmine said without thinking.

Her eyes widened when she realized what she'd just said. She went to apologize but saw the corners of Amira's mouth lift as if she were about to laugh.

"You aren't shit," Amira chuckled. "It's way too soon."

"It slipped!" Jazmine laughed.

One thing she could count on her girls for was a good laugh. No matter the circumstances or situation, none of them liked to see one another down for too long. Really, not at all. This was just a rough patch Amira was going through. They'd all been through them and more than likely would again. It wasn't about how you got there but what you'd do to get out of it.

"Yeah, yeah. I wasn't about to play with that man, and he wasn't about to play with me or my money," Amira said.

"Right," Quinn said. "Taking him to court was the best thing. Do you have to keep paying rent?"

"Who?" Amira asked incredulously. "That man isn't getting another damn penny out of me. And I better get my deposit back, too."

Mr. Fletcher and anyone else who thought she was paying rent when she had to move were out of their minds.

"You sure better, or I'ma have Keenan pay him a little visit," Jazmine said.

Her long-time boyfriend, one of her *lil' friends* from back in the day, considered Amira family. All Jazmine had to do was give him a name. Amira wasn't trying to get anyone else involved in her mess. Hopefully, now, Mr. Fletcher knew she was the wrong one to play with. Amira finished eating her last wing and zoned out of the conversation.

Her mind wandered to what she thought her life was supposed to look like at thirty-one. She had a good-paying job as a case manager, friends who loved and supported her, more than a few stamps on her passport, intact health, and, before today, a roof over her head. Yet, Amira knew some-thing...someone was missing.

She was content with the life she'd created but that hadn't always been the case. Daydreams of being married, starting her own family, traveling the world, and breaking generational curses had once been the only thing she thought about. It had once been what she knew was destined for her. She'd pushed the ideas so far out of her mind over the years that the thought of it happening now was almost comical.

"Amira," Quinn said, snapping her out of her daze.

"Huh? What'd you say?"

Quinn squinted. "What were you just over there thinking about?"

She shook her head, not wanting to expose herself or her intrusive thoughts. But then, she decided to share because she wanted to hear their perspective.

"Are y'all happy with where y'all are in life?" Amira asked.

Jazmine licked chicken crumbs from her fingers and nodded. "I am."

"At this very moment, yes," Quinn answered.

"So, there's nothing y'all would change?"

They pondered for a beat, and Quinn answered first. "I don't regret having Journey by any means, but I wish I would've waited until I was a bit older."

Four years Amira's junior, Quinn considered

herself more of a sibling than a cousin. Her mama, Sonya, had practically raised Amira. The only time they weren't attached at the hip was when Amira went away to college. Not having her big cousin physically around to keep an eye on her resulted in Quinn having the prettiest little girl at age seventeen.

"With the way Auntie used to be on us about getting pregnant, I just knew you'd stay a virgin forever." She chuckled.

"Girl." Quinn sighed. "She cried for months when I told her. You see, I was one and done, though."

Amira nodded. "Mhm. You can still give Journey a sibling."

"And start all over? I'll pass." Quinn chuckled.

Journey had enough cousins on both sides of her family to compensate for a sibling. Quinn couldn't fathom having a baby right now. Her answer about being happy would most definitely change if she were.

"What about you?" Jazmine asked Amira.

"You asking if I want a baby?"

Jazmine shook her head. "No. Are you happy with where you are in life? You asked us that out of the blue, so I know there's more on your mind."

And there was. It always was.

"Honestly... I don't know," she answered truthfully, pausing to let her words settle. She hadn't been honest with herself in a while. "I'm just... living, you know? Existing. I had it mapped out in my mind that by the time I was thirty, I'd be married with a few kids and a life of ease. Comfort. Something worth mentioning."

Quinn's throat produced an ache, hearing her cousin sound so down. "You have so many great things worth mentioning, Mira. Just because it hasn't happened yet doesn't mean it can't or it won't."

"I just feel like I'm running out of time. Like I've missed out on so much by listening to Auntie Sonya and everyone else," Amira admitted.

Frowning, Quinn's forehead creased. "What is that supposed to mean?"

"Out of everyone in our family, your mama and a few other women we were around growing up, stayed in our ear about not focusing on men. To get a degree, secure stability in our lives, and not get tied down so young by a man."

"Yeah, and? No one said you had to listen," Quinn stated. She loved her mama, Sonya, but she didn't run her life.

"But I did, and I'm paying the price for it," Amira said.

Jazmine cleared her throat. "Hold on, now. You think that the women who played a part in raising you are the reason your life didn't turn out as planned?"

"Not necessarily the sole reason, but yes." Amira shrugged, emotions going haywire.

Shaking her head, Quinn locked her phone after reading a text. "You can't blame them for that, Mira. That's not fair. They were only telling us what they thought was best."

"And I get that. I do, but I wish I wouldn't have listened. At least not to some advice," Amira said.

She always second-guessed herself and her decisions, and she knew it was because of how they were raised. While Quinn rebelled and did her own thing, Amira played it safe. She was never heavily influenced by the temptation of the unknown.

"Personally," Jazmine began, "I don't think there's anything wrong with what they said. We've witnessed it before. Women put their all into everyone and everything else, especially men, and don't have anything to fall back on when things go wrong. They weren't lying."

"And even if they were, as women, we have to understand that it's perfectly fine to be a go-getter with or without a man. That ambition is either in you or it isn't. How you prioritize reaching your goals and balancing life outside of them is up to you. You think because I had Journey that life was supposed to stop?"

Amira shook her head. "No, and I'm proud of you for not letting it."

"Thank you, but it's because I learned to balance it all. Yes, I had goals I didn't accomplish and dreams I didn't fulfill because I had a child so young with a man who promised us the world, but not once did I let my circumstances or a man dictate my happiness. My mama and, hell, probably yours, too, did. I couldn't put that pressure on myself or my baby. She didn't deserve that and neither do you," Quinn said.

One thing Amira loved about her cousin was how she never held her tongue. She gathered her with the utmost respect and love. It was never her intention to make Amira feel bad about her choices in life but to make her view things from a different perspective. Quinn knew that had she listened and obeyed half of what her mama told her, she wouldn't have been here today—some things in life you had to figure out on your own.

"Also," Quinn said, and Jazmine stopped her.

"Okay, Professor Q. I think she gets it." She snickered.

Amira smirked. "It's fine. I'm listening."

Quinn flipped her tongue out at Jazmine and continued, "Like I was saying... I get focusing on yourself and everything. We still hear that to this day. But at some point, you can't let outside influences sway how you feel and how you want your life to go. If that includes a man, so be it. Everyone's realities are different. Why would you ever take advice from someone you don't want to end up like?"

"Oop. I heard that," Jazmine said.

Amira heard her, too. She had made some valid points. The thing was, Quinn's words of advice had come much too late. The topic changed, but Jazmine and Quinn both knew what was up. Amira wasn't necessarily sad about how her life had turned out but who it hadn't included.

She earned the degrees, secured a career, had a plush savings account, a retirement plan, and somewhat accomplished everything the women in her life advised her to focus on. The only thing missing was him.

Breaking up with Saleem was the one thing Amira regretted. So, no. She wasn't happy, and since she was being honest... she hadn't been for years.

"DO YOU NOT HAVE FAITH IN YOUR FUTURE?"

TWO

"Look, I'm not in the mood to play with you today. I just left the gym, and I'm trying to enjoy my smoothie."

Saleem couldn't help but smirk, overhearing one of his loyal customers on the phone. He could expect to see her face three days out of the week, ordering the same smoothie or juice. From observation and brief conversations they shared, he knew she wasn't to be played with.

"How's that juice tasting, Mr. Richie?" Saleem asked another customer.

The older gentleman with gray locs nodded and held the drink out in front of him. "Not too bad. That ginger really does have some kick to it, but I like it. I can get used to it."

Chuckling, Saleem agreed. "Yeah. It'll catch you off guard. That's the juice of the week."

"Keep it on the menu," Mr. Richie said.

Nodding while pushing in a chair, Saleem said, "Will do."

That week, Mr. Richie was the fourth person who'd requested to keep the juice on the menu permanently. Saleem liked to switch it up weekly, monitor the feedback and sales of each one, and adjust the menu accordingly. As a successful busi-nessman, it was only right to give the people what they wanted.

Mr. Richie always came by after his daily laps around the strip mall. Most people who stopped by Jennie Mae's Juicery were frequent visitors who put others on about the place. Countless weekends spent with his grandmother, Jennie Mae, had shaped Saleem into the man he is today. Though he used to complain about having to pick fresh fruits and vegetables from the garden with his sisters and brother, Saleem cherished those moments.

Jennie Mae had been ahead of her time. She promoted healthy living within her community and believed in the power of nature to heal. She always had. Saleem couldn't recall a time in his adolescence and teenage years when he or anyone in their immediate family got sick. And, if they did, Jennie Mae had a remedy. She was a pillar in not just their neighborhood but around the city.

Before Jennie Mae was called home in her late eighties, Saleem promised to continue sharing her knowledge and keep her legacy alive. At the time, in his mid-twenties in grad school and recovering from a breakup he never saw coming, Saleem didn't know how he'd continue making her proud. The pressure of not failing at any aspect of his life almost took him out, but he prevailed.

The idea to start a business in her name didn't hit him until one of his closest friends, Najee, hit him up about an herbal tea Jennie Mae once made him drink when he was sick. That was his opportunity right there, and Saleem took it. He started small, making juices in his kitchen with the help of his sisters, then expanded on a grander scale.

A greater demand called for a larger space, bringing everything his grandmother taught him to a bigger audience, especially in underserved communities where access to fresh, healthy food options was scarce. Now, there were three main locations throughout the city. The one Saleem was currently at was the last location to open.

Juices could be bought from coffee shops, hospitals, sports arenas, small businesses in the region, and a well-known multinational supermarket chain sold them in stores worldwide.

Jennie Mae's wasn't just a million-dollar business to Saleem. It was a way to reconnect with his roots on both sides of his family, honor Jennie Mae, and offer something meaningful to the community. He was leaving his mark and ensuring his grandmother's remained. Some of her infamous recipes and pictures of her adorned the space, reminding Saleem daily that every sacrifice he'd made to get here was worth it.

"I'ma be in my office if y'all need me," Saleem announced to the crew working.

They nodded, telling him okay. Heading toward the back of the store, Saleem felt his phone vibrate. *Perfect timing,* he thought, stepping into his office. Closing the door, he answered the phone and followed the instructions he'd heard more than he liked from the prerecorded woman. Saleem placed the call on speaker as he sat down. The prison's background noise of muffled chatter and the clank of cell doors filtered through the receiver before Najee's voice could.

"Aye. What's good, bro," he said, making Saleem smirk.

His upbeat tone sounded like he was in a good mood today.

"What's the deal? You called at the perfect time," Saleem said.

"Yeah? Fuck you got going on?"

Saleem woke up the screen on his iMac and unlocked it. "Business as usual. Same shit, different day."

"Getting new money a different way," Najee recited, finishing off one of the sayings they quoted since they were teenagers.

"You know what it is. You straight, though?" Saleem asked.

On the other end of the phone, Najee glanced over his shoulder. Nothing in prison was private, not even conversations he thought no one could hear.

"Yeah. Shit's all good. Ain't too much complaining a nigga can do up in here." He chuckled somberly. "Time gon' move regardless."

Saleem smirked. Even in the deepest currents, Najee found a way to keep his head above water.

"And ain't gon' slow down," Saleem agreed. "You'll be home in a minute."

"Longest minute of my life, bro." Najee chuckled and got serious. "Real shit, though... how my ma been holding up? I try not to call and worry her."

Najee called his great Aunt Joyce, Ma, for a reason. She raised him as her own, and no one could tell her shit about her baby. She didn't hide her disappointment when he got locked up for violating his probation, but it was for a good cause. Still, out of respect for her sanity, Najee kept his phone calls few and far between. Thankfully, Saleem was like a nephew to her, so he could still keep tabs on her.

"I talked to her this morning. Gon' swing by there in a few days. You know she hates being checked on." Saleem chuckled.

Najee smirked. He knew it all too well but didn't care what she hated. "She be fronting. Knowing if we didn't, she'd put her foot up our ass."

"And then say we made her do it." Saleem laughed.

The line quieted, and he knew Najee was thinking about how much time he had left in there. That's what prison did; it gave him nothing but time to think. Seconds, minutes, hours, and days he didn't even know. Trying to keep count would make the stay seem longer than it already was. He was months in on a year and some change charge the judge wasn't lenient on, and Najee was over the shit already. But he didn't regret why he was there at all.

"You already know," he said and cleared his

throat. "Once I'm out, that shit we talked about is a go. I was ready before, but now I'm about to go full throttle wit' it."

The optimism and hype in his voice made Saleem proud.

He nodded, even though Najee couldn't see him. "Only way to do it. This ain't shit but a minor setback. Keep your head on straight in there and stay out the way. You know niggas in there don't have much to lose and will try to keep you locked down wit' em'."

Saleem wasn't saying anything Najee didn't already know, but he appreciated the reminder. Some days, especially on the bad ones, he was ready to knock a nigga's head off their shoulders. Adding more time to his sentence and creating unnecessary beef because he couldn't control his emotions wasn't part of Najee's plans.

Chuckling, Najee said, "You on this bitch soundin' like a motivational speaker. You gon' write a self-help book for me to read while I drink a juice?"

"Fuck you, bruh." Saleem laughed, shaking his head. "If I wrote a book, it'd do numbers. You might be onto something."

It was no secret that whatever Saleem touched turned gold. Well, mostly everything. He was a natural-born hustler. If the money on the table aligned with his beliefs, he was sitting down to count it by hand.

"Shit, I might be. But, for real... I 'preciate you."

He knew he didn't need to tell him every time they talked but Najee did. Saleem was his brother. They weren't related by blood but bonded by it.

"It's nothing," Saleem replied without hesitation. "Ain't shit changed but the day."

"Bet that," Najee said, his voice steady. "I'ma let you go and call Renae 'fore she be trippin' on her next visit."

Saleem smirked, knowing his girlfriend would be on one if he didn't hit her line. "Yeah, gon' head and handle that. And don't worry about Auntie. She good," he reassured.

The last thing he wanted was for him to be in there worried about her.

"A'ight. Be safe out there."

"Always."

The call ended, and Saleem stared at the screen until it blacked out. Exhaling, he focused on the unread emails waiting for him. Najee's trip to prison was so unexpected, and out of the blue, it took everyone by surprise. Not Saleem, though. The life they used to live was embedded in their

DNA, and considering the circumstances... Najee had every reason to bring the past out of him. He was only in the wrong because he violated his probation.

It was all good, though. Saleem was going to make sure his re-entry into the world greeted him with more money and was as smooth as possible. By mid-afternoon, Saleem was ready to wrap his day up. He was an early riser, waking up before the sun most mornings, and his day didn't typically slow down until late in the evening. It was one thing to own a business and another to be invested in it on all ends.

Stepping from the hallway into the lobby, Saleem frowned. He tried to keep the atmosphere in Jennie Mae's as chill and relaxing as possible. That included the warm earth-tone colors, wooden chairs, the chalkboard wall with vibrant hand-drawn art by a local artist, and most importantly, the music. Saleem liked to keep it family-friendly with the tunes, so the boisterous explicit rap lyrics ricocheting off the walls had him vexed.

"Aye," he called out, the bass in his voice immediately capturing the employees on shift. "Y'all 'bouta do a drill or something? Turn something else on."

"You don't listen to EST Gee?" one of the young boys, Lune, asked while grinning.

Saleem couldn't help but chuckle. "Yeah, in my free time. Not while I'm at work. Then, you playing the explicit version."

Removing his plastic gloves, Lune dug in the pocket of his jeans to retrieve his phone. He paused the song, then disconnected his phone from the Bluetooth system. Tossing the gloves in the trash, he smirked.

"We all good now. Saige acting like she couldn't hook hers up, so I did." Lune shrugged.

"I told you my phone was about to die!" Saige said. "Hey, Saleem."

His head bobbed upward in a nod. "What's going on, Saige? It's just two of y'all today?"

"No. Damari went to the restroom. Jess called in sick," Saige answered.

Saleem nodded. "A'ight. How these two get on the same schedule?" he asked as Damari headed from the back where the restrooms were located.

He and Lune were brothers and what the shift manager on duty, Kayla, considered a pain in her ass. She was in the manager's office now, going over the schedule. There had to have been a mistake. Kayla never scheduled them at the same time.

Rolling her eyes, Saige shrugged. "Who knows? You know they're some finessers."

Damari mushed her in the head before slapping hands with Saleem. "Shut up, lying. What up?"

"That's what I'm trying to figure out," Saleem said, chuckling. "Y'all don't be on no BS on the clock."

"Nah. We ain't on that," Lune defended.

Saleem believed him... now anyway. Damari was the first to start working there, and when his brother got in a bind and needed a place to work, he put him on. Lune wasn't keen on the typical nine-to-five jobs like everyone else his age. He was more so into hustling and living the kind of life that laced his pockets with bands by the hour instead of double digits. Sometimes, that involved extracurricular activities that hid his identity while a Glock 19 occupied his hand. But he was trying to live right, even if temporarily, and Saleem respected that. As long as that respect was reciprocated, all was good.

"A'ight. Saige, it's a charger near the freezer," Saleem said. "Turn on some music that won't have folks in here trying to get us shut down."

Saige beamed. "Thank you, and okay!"

Lune smirked and bumped Damari's shoulder. "We'll put their ass out first."

"Be coo', man," Saleem said, chuckling. "I'm out."

Damari chucked the deuces while greeting a fly-ass chick with workout gear on. Jennie Mae's had all potential prospects if you were single and on your fitness kick. Saleem had fallen victim a time or two to women who claimed their workout session wasn't enough. Burning more calories with his dick buried inside them sounded much more appealing. So, he signed them up for two-a-days, not caring if their bodies recovered properly from the vigorous routine he took them through.

Saleem greeted a few people on the walk to his SUV. Seeing the packed shopping center parking lot never got old. When Cree, his close friend, first mentioned buying the property, Saleem was on board. He and a few other men in their circle invested, and their profit hadn't slowed down since.

After whipping through the city and checking on his other locations, Saleem hit the gym. He hadn't had time to go on his morning run, so he got a quick workout in before heading to his parents' house. His cell rang the second he shifted gears, parking the vehicle in their massive driveway.

"Must be that time of the year," Saleem said once he picked up.

Humored giggles came from the caller. "Don't be that way," Brandi said.

"You in town?" Saleem asked.

He was being the only way they both knew him to be, which was straightforward.

"Not yet. I will be in a few days, though, and I *need* to see you," Brandi stated, her voice lust-filled.

That's all it'd ever been between them since graduate school; months after Saleem concluded that he and Amira were no longer a thing. The shit...stung, and Brandi was there on her knees or her back, and sometimes her side when he let her spend the night, to help soothe the pain. Saleem appreciated her efforts and her pussy.

"Text me when you land," he said, opening his door.

"You're coming to get me from the airport?"

The hopefulness in her tone almost made him chuckle. Brandi had misinterpreted his words.

"Do you want me to?" Saleem asked, stepping inside the house.

Warmth and cinnamon embraced him as he slipped his shoes off by the door. Brandi paused, considering his offer. She didn't know why this month, day, or year would be any different between them. He seldom requested her presence now but never turned her down when she yearned to be in his space. Brandi had family in the city, and him...sometimes. Saleem didn't count as hers just because they linked up once or twice every three months.

"If you need a ride, I can arrange for someone to pick you up," Saleem offered, figuring her silence was telling him no.

"Yeah, sure," she agreed. "So you won't have to go out of your way. I'll text you my flight information."

Saleem didn't need that but said, "A'ight. It's been a minute since we kicked it."

Brandi smiled. It'd been four months... not that she was counting or anything. He wasn't either and never would. Saleem could go months without sex. His discipline had always been a trait that he was proud of. It created a sense of control, making him not be swayed by fleeting emotions but by intentional choices.

Saleem was stingy with his dick, and he had every right to be. If a woman was privileged enough to get it, he considered it an honor—a reward. Luck had been on her side. Being attractive wasn't enough for him.

"Yeah, it has. I can't wait to see you, too."

He smirked. She never could wait. Saleem told

her to have a safe flight and a good rest of her day before hanging up. Sliding his phone into the pocket of his sweatpants, he entered the kitchen where his mama, Tiffany, and his sister, Tayah, were. She sat at the dining table with her MacBook open, working as usual, and a glass of her favorite wine not far out of reach.

"What's good, sis?" Saleem greeted her first with a kiss on the cheek.

Tayah made him stay in place as she wrapped her arms around his waist. He let her know he'd just left the gym, but she didn't care about a bit of sweat. She hugged him tightly, rocking them side-to-side.

"I've missed you," Tayah said, releasing him.

"I missed you, too."

Like the big brother he was, Saleem examined her face. Tayah's usual fair brown skin, a shade lighter than Saleem's, had been sun-kissed. She was glowing with a tan she missed during the winter months. Her work trip out of the country, which mainly was play, could take all the credit for how radiant she looked.

Not a dark brown strand of hair was out of place on her head. When she returned home, the first thing Tayah did was book a hair appointment with her sister. She loved her curls, but silk presses owned her heart. Saleem lifted her hand to see if anything was different; if anything stood out.

Tayah chuckled. "Please, do not start. Mama, get your son."

He smirked. "I'm just looking. You were gone for a minute. Had to make sure some lame didn't get any bright ideas."

"The only person who needs to be worried about something on their finger is you." Tayah snickered.

Ignoring her, Saleem walked over to his mama. He greeted her with the same affection, kissing her forehead while pulling her five-foot-seven frame into a hug.

"What's up, Mama."

"Not much. Fixing us a bite to eat. You want some?" Tiffany asked.

Saleem eyed the contents on the counter, knowing he wasn't about to pass up one of her infamous salmon and rice bowls. He wasn't sure how she made them taste as good as she did, but they were always a hit.

"Of course. Gon' hook me up one," Saleem said. "What y'all been over here doing?"

He placed his phones on the table and sat down. If his days didn't get too hectic, Saleem made it a priority to stop by his parents' crib. As the oldest, at thirty-four, laying eyes on them was non-negotiable. With his father, Youssef, out of town, Saleem knew his mama didn't mind the company. She didn't at all and loved it when any of her quartet of children stopped by.

"Catching up," Tayah said.

"As if we didn't talk almost every day while you were there." Tiffany chuckled.

Saleem glanced his mama's way, the corners of his mouth lifting. She looked so at peace. Had they not celebrated her birthday months prior, Saleem would bet money that she wasn't almost sixty but in her early thirties like Tayah.

With her lustrous dark brown skin, striking cheekbones, tightly coiled curls in a pixie cut, and gentle smile, Tiffany Majid was the epitome of beauty—externally and internally. According to her husband, it was love at first sight, and he wanted to bear witness to her beauty for the rest of his life. That declaration was made when Youssef was eighteen and had just moved to the States.

He stepped inside her father's barbershop, needing a haircut, and left with a wife. Not that same day, of course, but within two years, Tiffany's last name was changed, and shortly after, she was pregnant with Saleem. Then came Tayah, another son,

Rahim, and the baby girl of the family, Yuhani, affectionately called Nini. Youssef saw it as an honor and a privilege to create a rich, multi-layered family.

They weren't just rich in wealth but in love, well-being, experiences, relationships, and purpose. So, yes. While she was vacationing on a beach in the middle of the winter, Tayah talked to her mama almost every day. She was Mama's girl through and through.

"I thought being a Velcro baby ended when you turned a certain age," Saleem teased.

Tayah rolled her brown eyes. "Yeah, well, it hasn't. You must've really missed me. You're on my head today," she said, chuckling.

Although they were only two years apart, they were the closest siblings. Their arguing and bickering as children was still prevalent but so was the love. Saleem still protected her like a hawk, and Tayah always had his back.

"That's nothing new. When I stop, be concerned," Saleem said and winked.

Tayah chuckled. "Of course."

Tiffany sat a steaming hot bowl down in front of him, then slid one in front of Tayah. She hooked both of theirs up with sweet chili salmon, cucumbers, fresh pico, avocado, corn, and green onions.

Saleem went to wash his hands before bowing his head to pray, and then dove in. He was in the middle of a bite when Tiffany brought up a topic that made Saleem almost lose his appetite.

"So," she began, "how's the wedding planning coming along?"

Tayah's eyes diverted his way, and she grinned. The grimace on his face was comical. Saleem took a moment to answer her loaded question.

"Y'all must have found me a bride," Saleem concluded.

"I hate to break it to you, but no… we haven't," Tiffany said.

Tayah cleared her throat. "Why haven't you is the better question."

Saleem had an answer but didn't feel like explaining. If anyone knew why he'd been dragging his feet about tying the knot, Tayah knew. As a Moroccan man, he was expected to marry and start a family. Culturally, it was frowned upon if you were a single man. You were looked at as less of a man the longer you jump from woman to woman with no real commitment. In Youssef's and some of their family members' eyes, Saleem didn't uphold marriage and family values.

He'd been getting by for years, and Youssef was

fed up. Saleem wasn't trying to disappoint his father or be considered a disgrace but getting married was harder than he thought. Not the task itself but finding a woman he deemed worthy of his devotion. His dad was going to stay upset if he thought Saleem was going to pick a random woman and give her his last name.

"You and I both know there ain't much out here," Saleem said, ready to change the subject.

"Is there not much out there, or have you gotten comfortable with being single?" Tiffany asked.

Saleem drank some water before saying, "Both. If a woman enters my life and I feel the urge to take care of her for the rest of our lives, then I'll act on those urges. Until then, I'm not rushing anything."

The mother-daughter duo connected eyes. Tayah tucked her lips to keep from saying what they were both thinking. Tiffany didn't. She was his mother and saw through the wall he was trying to keep up. It sounded good, but she knew better.

"And the house you got built is just going to do what... collect dust?" Tiffany wondered.

Years back, Saleem bought acres of land and built an immaculate home from the ground up. In his mind, that was the first step. The foundation. He'd been so focused on making Jennie Mae's

Juicery successful, that everything else got put on the back burner.

"Honestly, I should sell it," Saleem said.

Tayah's mouth dropped. "Nooo. Why would you do that? That home is gorgeous."

"I can just get another one built. I have time."

"Do you?" Tiffany chuckled.

She said it as if she knew something Saleem didn't, and that didn't sit right with him.

"I don't?" he asked.

Tiffany pursed her lips and continued eating as Tayah intervened. Saleem was talking crazy.

"Even if you don't, you could always fake it with someone. Have her sign an NDA. We won't tell Daddy," Tayah suggested.

Saleem glanced at his mama and knew that was a lie, at least for her. She didn't lie to her husband and keep secrets, especially regarding his beliefs. They'd gone through too much over the years, integrating their cultural and religious values into their household for that mess. Tiffany wasn't with it.

"Who is her, Tayah?" Saleem chuckled.

She shrugged passively. "I don't know. Somebody. You can't sit up here and tell us that you, my oh-so-handsome brother, have no woman you'd want to lock down?"

Saleem smirked at her compliment. "To give my last name and spend the rest of my life with? Absolutely not, and I really ain't in the mood to search."

Tiffany rolled her tongue over her teeth and sucked. "Hmm. Have we not raised you well? Do you not have faith in your future?"

"You've raised me perfectly," Saleem said, clearing that up quickly. "It's not about me having faith. It's about timing. My life is on the path it's supposed to be on. If I weren't meant to be married, have kids, and do the family thing, it would've happened by now. I'm not rushing the process."

"Well... you better. Your father will be home in less than three months, and he expects to attend a wedding."

"What?" Saleem uttered, confused. His bushy, thick brows dipped, creasing his forehead. His eyes bounced to Tayah, who was just as shocked before they pinned his mama in place. "What do you mean in less than three months? I thought he didn't come home until like June?"

Most of their family's wealth came from importing and exporting goods. Youssef had connections worldwide and had been traveling for the past year and a half to secure a significant deal that would set their family straight forever. Unbeknownst to his children, he'd be returning home sooner than he initially planned. Finalizations of the deal were being handled, and Youssef couldn't wait to get back to his family for good.

The last time he was home, Saleem thought he was joking when he said, "I'm looking forward to meeting my daughter-in-law when I return." For years, Youssef had thrown hints in his son's direction, even bragging about Saleem's male cousins, who they celebrated for settling down. Saleem thought they were on the same page about his difficulties, and he thought he had more time, but time was up.

"Nope," Tiffany said, standing up. "He'll be home soon, and you better not disappoint my husband."

Tayah snickered, and Saleem glared her way. "This shit ain't funny," he hissed lowly, sitting back in his seat. "Mama, you serious? Just because y'all got married—"

Tiffany turned away from the sink and shook her head, stopping whatever he was about to say. "Aht. Don't use us as an example. What you should've been doing was using your cousins as one. Every last one of them, well except for a few, are married, Saleem. This isn't something he's springing on you last minute. You've known since you were old enough to comprehend that as a man in this family, a man who was raised by a man who poured his blood, sweat, and tears into his home, that marriage wasn't something you could skip out on. So, there's no excuse as to why you haven't prepared to do the same."

He had a few reasons why, but none of them sounded valid enough against her tongue-lashing. Tiffany didn't feel sorry for him at all. Saleem had more than enough years to fulfill his obligations. Tayah wished she had more wine to sip. She never saw her brother as panicked as he was right now.

"I told you we could just make it up. Make Daddy think it's real," Tayah urged in a hushed tone.

Saleem closed his eyes as a headache breached. He valued not only his name but his family—their legacy. He wasn't sacrificing his dignity for a random woman. Youssef was lax about a lot of the traditions and beliefs of their blended families but marriage wasn't one of them. Though the expectation of marriage applied to only Moroccan men, he encouraged Tayah and Yuhani to honor their traditions and find a man who valued and loved them as he did their mother.

"Brandi isn't marriage material?" Tayah asked, making Saleem's eyes pop open.

"For another nigga? Sure. For me? Absolutely not."

Tayah huffed. She met the woman a few times…unexpectedly, but she didn't seem too bad.

"It'll be fake, though. You don't have to fall in love with her."

That L word made his nose crinkle and his eye twitch. Saleem shook his head.

"Nah. I'm not doing that. Daddy just gon' have to disown me."

Tayah knew then that he was really tripping. Saleem admired their father too much for him to be talking like that. *It has to be his nerves,* Tayah thought. Then, her mind ventured to the one woman from Saleem's past. The one who she believed was the cause of her brother keeping his heart to himself and not settling down.

"What if I help you out?" she suggested.

Saleem gave her a deadpan stare as Tiffany exited the kitchen. She had nothing else to say and hoped her son figured it out.

"And how do you plan on doing that?"

"I could reach out to… Amira." Tayah said her name so lowly that Saleem almost didn't hear her. But he had, and the delicious meal he had just finished eating threatened to decorate the table.

Her name hit him like a punch to the chest. Amira was the one who got away. The woman he'd spent years trying to forget, only to fail miserably every time her name crossed his mind or was mentioned. Tayah still kept up with her, but not in a, *let me see what she has going on for my brother*, type of way. They shared mutual friends on social media and showed love to one another.

Saleem stopped making himself miserable by keeping up with her years ago, which Tayah found oddly crazy, considering they were still connected in a way. They'd been inseparable in college, and Saleem was sure she was the one who would be his wife, but she had other plans. Ones that didn't involve him or his heart.

She insisted that he needed to live his life without the burden of a serious relationship. And now? He hadn't done shit but live with regret for letting her walk out of his life.

If she wasn't the one walking down the aisle to him, there wouldn't be a wedding. Saleem wasn't sure how Youssef would take that news, but it's the only news he had to deliver.

"I CAN TAKE CARE OF THAT... TAKE CARE OF YOU."

THREE

As tired as she was, the only thing on Amira's mind was going home once she clocked out of work for the day. Her to-do list was a mile long, and the extra days she'd been given to move were flying by. Three weeks had coasted by in the blink of an eye, yet she still hadn't found a place to move.

There were potential spots she looked at, but most of them had a waitlist that was months out. She didn't have that kind of time, nor did she want to rush into a quick lease and end up hating the place. Her options were few, but something had to shake. She wasn't trying to be on her Ginuwine tip by unblocking Chris and asking if he had room in his jeans.

Pulling into the driveway of the quaint, two-story home in the city, Amira parked her car. Christmas lights bordered the roof, and a Minnie Mouse inflatable dressed as Mrs. Claus made her smile. She'd been so out of whack with everything going on that she wasn't in the holiday spirit at all.

Maybe next year, she thought. Climbing out of her car, she grabbed a few bags from her trunk and headed to the front door. The heavily tinted burgundy Cadillac SUV she walked by made her lips purse out a whistle. It was clean, and she just knew Mrs. Peterson hadn't gone and bought her a new whip.

Amira knocked twice, and the door and screen door opened shortly after. As always, Mrs. Peterson greeted her with a smile. She looked forward to their bi-weekly visits, and her warm welcome was mainly the reason. She couldn't leave out her motherly advice and story times.

"Hey, sweetie. Come on in," Mrs. Peterson said.

Amira stepped inside, and soulful Christmas music was the first thing she heard. "Hi. How are you?"

Mrs. Peterson closed the door and waved her hand so she could follow her into the kitchen. Amira took in the large, spinning Christmas tree with gifts underneath, the stockings pinned to the mantel of the lit fireplace, and the sweet scent of caramel and peppermint.

"I'm doing just fine," Mrs. Peterson answered warmly. "How about you? I missed you the other week."

Amira sighed, placing the brown box and plastic bag of food on the counter. "I'm okay. I had so much going on. I still do, but I wasn't going to miss coming out to see you for a month."

Mrs. Peterson smiled. Although she had known Amira for only a few months, it felt like forever. One of the community programs Amira volunteered for gave away free food from a local farmer's market and weekly care packages to individuals and families who signed up. Mrs. Peterson wasn't above receiving the produce and meats. As she'd gotten older and didn't like leaving the house much, her trips to the store had lessened. Having someone bring groceries and necessities to her was a luxury she took advantage of.

"Well, thank you for thinking of little ole me," Mrs. Peterson said.

She reminded Amira of her grandmother; sweet as could be, with nothing but love packed into a small frame. Mrs. Peterson stayed fly, too. There wasn't a time Amira came over where she wasn't dressed to the nines with gold rings adorning her fingers, hair neatly done, and smelling expensive like she had somewhere to be. Amira found that adorable and admirable because she looked a hot mess nine times out of ten at the crib.

"Of course. Did you put up all the decorations by yourself?" Amira asked, placing the apples in the fruit basket.

"Oh, child, no." Mrs. Peterson chuckled. "I did what I could and had some help. Remind me to give you your gift before you go. Just in case I don't see you next week."

Amira paused. "Mrs. Peterson, you didn't have to get me anything."

"I didn't have to, but I did. You've done so much for me over the months and keep me company. What's a little gift going to hurt, huh?"

Tears pricked her eyes, and Amira quickly blinked them away. It wasn't unusual for her to get emotional by someone's genuine consideration, but it'd been a rough month. Mrs. Peterson had no idea how much she appreciated her. Besides bringing her food and dinner, Amira helped tidy up around her home some days. She sniffled and tried shaking the onset of tears threatening to show just how drained she was.

"I could feel the heaviness on you as soon as you walked in," Mrs. Peterson said, rubbing her back. "Come on over here and sit down so we can talk."

Amira blew out a deep breath. "Okay."

She took a seat at the round oakwood table. Poinsettia placemats and Christmas tree dinnerware sets filled the spaces. Mrs. Peterson went all out for the holidays and enjoyed every bit of it. So, seeing Amira down in the dumps had her concerned.

"Now, who do I need to give a good cursing out to?"

Amira chuckled, appreciating her for lightening the mood. "You be cursing folks out?"

"Not as often as I used to, but they can still get it," she said, pursing her lips painted a dark brown hue.

"I heard that," Amira said, then sighed.

She gave Mrs. Peterson the rundown of her hectic life, leaving no detail behind except for Chris' shortcomings. He wasn't worth mentioning at all... ever again.

"So, that's what's been going on with me. All over the place and trying to hold it together." Amira laughed to keep from bawling. She'd been doing that a lot lately.

"You don't have to hold it together. Let me know what you need, baby. There's no use in stressing about something out of your control, but you don't have to figure it out alone."

Her words melted Amira's heart. Rapid blinks cleared her wet, blurry vision.

"I don't know what you could give me to make this ordeal smoother. I mean, unless you have a place for me to stay," she said jokingly.

Mrs. Peterson smiled. "I might. Let me make a few phone calls and see."

Amira's eyes lit up. "Really?"

"Mhm." Mrs. Peterson patted her hand. "You're not the only one with connections around here."

They laughed, and Amira exhaled. If Mrs. Peterson came through for her, she wouldn't know how to repay her, but there'd be no need for that.

"I see," she said, then frowned, hearing what sounded like a drill. "Someone doing construction nearby?"

"Oh, that's my nephew. He's been over here getting my guest bedroom together for company," Mrs. Peterson said.

"That's nice of him. I stopped by Freddy's to grab dinner for us. There's extra if he wants some."

The mom-and-pop soul food diner had been

around for years and was a staple in the city. They closed down some months back due to the wife's health, but they were back like they never left. Amira couldn't wait to eat her baked macaroni and cheese and yams together.

"You can go ask him and see," Mrs. Peterson said, adjusting her glasses while flipping through a worn book filled with numbers. "I wonder if ol' Billy's number is still the same. She used to sell homes," she mumbled, making Amira grin.

She stood from the table and headed to where the noise came from. Since coming to Mrs. Peterson's house, she hadn't met any of her family... hardly heard about them, so she was excited to meet whoever was helping her out. Making it down the hallway, Amira stood outside the closed bedroom door and squinted.

The Christmas tunes had faded, replaced by a song that Amira had played on repeat more than a few times. She could've written the lyrics herself had she been that kind of artist—one who made her want to inject every song she'd penned into her veins. Instead of knocking, she swayed and lip-synced the soulful lyrics Alex Isley belted out over her verse on *Same Mistake*. She and Destin Conrad were a lethal collaboration on a track, and Amira felt every word.

Not wanting the drill to start back up before she could make her presence known, she knocked and took a slight step back. The music stopped, and when the door opened, so did Amira's breathing. Her heart decided to follow suit.

It was as if she'd entered a different world. A past life of only them... only him. Somehow, with no vital organ, Amira could still move her feet. She backpedaled into the wall behind her and clutched her chest.

"I need you to breathe."

His voice. Its depth and maturity flooded her ears in modest waves, slightly bringing her back to shore. Or wherever it took her when he spoke. Then, she felt his hands. They cradled her round face like they did that dreadful day in her dorm. That was the last day Amira felt his touch, breathed his air, and looked him in the eyes. *Am I dreaming?* Her brain was short-circuiting. Slowly, she placed her hands atop his and exhaled a stuttered breath with a word attached.

"Saleem.

His name on her lips made Saleem want to kiss her. He *always* wanted to kiss her worries away.

Right now, he was her concern. She whispered his name so softly it felt like a secret code being exchanged, as if the air itself might snatch him away if it heard her.

"Angel," Saleem said.

Her hands fell, and the distance she placed between them returned. Amira looked around the hallway, confusion smacking her in the face.

"I have to be tripping right now," Amira mumbled, taking him in.

It was a lot to take in. He looked *good*. Too damn good, and it pissed her off how easily he still had this effect on her. It wasn't fair. Saleem was, hands down, the finest man she ever laid eyes on. This wasn't the young man she remembered from back then.

No, Saleem was *all* man. A *grown* fucking man with defined muscles that teased her from underneath a white Polo tee. Time had done nothing to dim his presence. His neatly trimmed beard framed a strong jawline that only enhanced his striking features. Those full pink-brown lips of his had kissed and talked Amira through plenty of orgasms and hours of phone conversations.

Coal-black hair was pulled into a neat bun, settling at his tattooed nape. She always loved his hair and was glad he hadn't cut it. Amira was sure he'd still look fine without it, though. His deep-set eyes told a story she'd been left out of; pages ripped from the seams, leaving her to make up her own before the tale continued. They were soulful and intense, as if he could see straight through her all the way down to the regrets she didn't want to admit. Like her, his heart just realized it needed to function.

"You're not tripping at all," Saleem said.

But... he was over the fact that Amira... his Angel, was standing before him as if she'd just walked out of heaven. Or had they been in hell this entire time? Saleem wasn't sure, but there had to be a reason she was here, looking like every bit of the woman he knew she'd grow up to be. Physically, at least. He'd tap into the other parts he'd missed out on, later.

Amira's curves in the cream sweater dress were relentless. Saleem let his eyes roam, snapshotting each dip to memory. She was much thicker than the twenty-year-old he helped put some weight on. Baby girl was a brick house, possessing plush thighs, the sexiest hip-dips, and an ass he couldn't see from the front, but Saleem knew it was there.

I bet that mothafucka is still soft, too, he thought, then smirked before focusing on her face.

It was fuller, with eyes that stared back at him like he was unreal. Her nervousness radiated from her body, but it emanated intrigue, too. She had a million questions that Saleem was ready to answer because he had a few of his own. Her hair favored his in a high ponytail. The tips of her wavy strands she'd curled that morning and that one coiled loc brushed between her shoulders.

Gotdamn, she's gorgeous, Saleem thought to himself. He was tongue-tied at her beauty, and the pictures he came across or was sent by Tayah had nothing on her in real-time.

"Um," Amira said and chuckled nervously. "Hello."

His sexy lips quirked in a smirk. "Damn, hello to you, too."

Without warning, he pulled her into his sturdy chest, wrapping her in a hug that turned Amira into putty. Her body transitioned to a body-shuddering vortex that weakened and awakened her. SWV knew what the hell they were singing about because Amira was losing balance. She wasn't expecting the hug but didn't pull away.

Arms circled his waist, and she inhaled, breathing in his mind-numbing smell. Her senses were overwhelmed by a fragrance redolent of the bold, smooth, addictive man he was. Saleem rarely wore cologne. He preferred body oils that fused deliciously with his natural scent. A mix of slightly sweet musk, a woodsy vanilla, with hints of citrus that would indeed cling to her senses, skin, and the atmosphere when they parted ways.

Amira was seconds away from telling him how much she missed him when Mrs. Peterson's voice interrupted their reunion. Reluctantly, Saleem let her go... for now. It'd been far too long since he felt her in his arms, and now that he had again, he wasn't letting her get away.

"Your aunt wanted me to ask if you were hungry," Amira said. "I brought us dinner."

He nodded, refraining from saying the lewd words on the tip of his tongue where he wanted her instead. Food, though he was starving, could wait. He knew she hadn't been pleased correctly in some time. It was all in the way her arousal seeped from her pores.

I can take care of that... take care of you. Saleem was ready for whatever. He'd take her down right in this hallway if she let him. Amira noticed the solicitous glint in his eyes, and she swallowed hard.

"Okay," she said lowly, easing away from him and down the hall. "I hope you're okay with ribs. That's what she likes."

"I don't eat meat."

She paused at his words before he continued.

"I'm not eating it this week," he added. "But I can make an exception."

Amira smirked, and she wanted to turn around to see the look on his face. She wouldn't see it, though, because his eyes were glued to her *meaty* ass. He'd eaten that plenty and would break his fast on the spot for a taste.

She kept walking, damn near running toward the kitchen. Suddenly, she wanted to remove every article of clothing she had on. It was hot!

"Did you find him?" Mrs. Peterson teasingly asked.

"Y-Yes. We were talking."

Amira hurriedly peeled her straw open and shoved it into her white foam cup. Parched, she downed the ice-cold water, uncaring about the look Mrs. Peterson gave her. She'd be thirsty, too, if a man snatched her breath away, forcing all fluids in her body to navigate to the seat of her thong.

"Well, that's good you two got acquainted," Mrs. Peterson smiled.

Saleem entered the kitchen, eyes landing on Amira. He smirked, and she reclaimed her seat before she dropped to her knees and showed him that she, too, would make an exception to eat some meat. *I just know his dick still tastes good,* she thought and grinned.

"Auntie Joyce, I didn't know you knew my Amira."

Her eyes shot up to him. Saleem staked claim on her so smoothly, Mrs. Peterson didn't even peep it.

"Oh, yes! She's just the sweetest thing. That son of mine signed me up for the program she volunteers at," she said.

"Yeah? That's what's up. You know Najee gon' always make sure you're straight."

"As are you. How do you two know one another?"

Her question was innocently asked, but it was heavy—too heavy to answer in this enclosed space. Saleem responded in the best, respectable way he could.

"We had a thing going on some years back, but the timing wasn't right."

Amira stared at him, not believing he just said that. But he hadn't lied. The timing... according to her, wasn't right. The way he enunciated the word *thing* tightened her chest. As if what they shared meant nothing. She couldn't blame him, though. Their *thing* was no longer because of her.

"And look at God, connecting you two again,"

Joyce said, and then it dawned on her. "Wait a second. You're the one he—"

"Auntie, chill," Saleem urged, chuckling.

Amira's eyes darted between them. Joyce wore a knowing smirk, while Saleem looked... bashful? Not embarrassed because he knew the conversations he and Joyce shared, and he meant every word conversed. She questioned him about marriage, too, like Tiffany. Not because she knew he had obligations but because Joyce knew he wanted to be a husband, unlike Najee.

"I was just saying. I'm going to mind my business." She snickered. "But you know what they say about old love returning."

Amira wasn't sure she wanted to know, but Saleem was interested in her outlook.

"No one's ever told me what it means," he said.

"There's some unfinished business there. The timing may not have been right before, but here's a second chance. You're single, right, baby?" Joyce asked Amira.

She nodded.

"See. So is Saleem. Surely, y'all can work some things out."

Her suggestion sounded hopeful and not like a suggestion at all. It was more like a statement, and she dared either of them to put up a rebuttal. Saleem was all for that if she was. He glanced her way, and Amira held his gaze before smiling. She'd placed their relationship on pause, but had it truly ended?

Finally getting to the reason they came to the kitchen, the trio ate. Saleem was amused by the way Amira dug into her food without trying to look cute in his presence. Fine as hell or not, her stomach was touching her back. She didn't say much while they shared the unexpected meal. Thankfully, Joyce had plenty to talk about. When they were finished, Saleem stood with his empty plate and looked down at her.

Amira glanced upward, envy residing in her eyes and wonderment at how they'd gotten here after years of no contact. Over the years, when she missed him the most, she'd venture to his social media pages that he hardly used. She wanted to see how life had been treating him without her, and it was abundantly clear that it was marvelous. The man was standing in front of her, glowing from the inside out.

"Yes?" she questioned when he said nothing.

Saleem pointed to her empty plate, dirtied napkins, and greased stained cup. "Are you finished?"

"Oh. Yeah... yes," Amira quipped, forgetting that in his presence, she didn't touch trash. Nor a door. Or her money. Or the ground if her feet hurt. Utterly disgusted by her lack of remembrance, Saleem grabbed the waste and headed toward the bin on the other side of the kitchen. Amira looked on as he used his foot to lift the lid, dump everything inside, and then pivot to wash his hands at the sink.

Her breaths quickened, watching the flex of his veins with each scrub. She also noticed a few tattoos decorating his arm and an eye-crossing white gold diamond watch with a black leather band on his wrist. It was subtle but a pretty penny. Amira didn't realize she was rubbing her wrist, wondering if she should treat herself to some new jewelry until Saleem addressed her.

Drying his hands, he said, "Piaget."

Her brows pinched. "Huh?"

"The brand of my watch. You want one?"

No holds barred. If she said yes, even if she didn't say yes, Saleem was buying her one.

"No. Was just admiring it. It's nice," she said.

Saleem's head bobbed forward. "Thank you. Auntie, I'ma finish up and be out your hair for the day. You good?"

"Yes. I appreciate you for getting the place together."

So, he helped with the decorations, Amira concluded.

"You're welcome. You know it's nothing."

Saleem gathered her trash now that she was finished. He needed to busy himself before Amira had him lose more track of time. He was supposed to have been gone.

"Well, Billy's number changed," Joyce said, snapping Amira out of her daydream. "I was hoping she had some ready-to-move-in spots for you. We can still keep searching."

Amira ran a hand over the back of her neck and sighed. She wished Joyce hadn't said anything about her situation until Saleem was out of earshot, but unfortunately, he'd heard every word.

"You need a place to stay?" he asked sincerely.

"No."

Joyce waved her off and faced Saleem. "Don't listen to her. That asshole of a landlord done put her out for no reason. Can you believe he did that?"

"Mrs. Peterson, seriously. I'm okay. I've been looking at places. I go tour one tomorrow," Amira said, wanting the attention to be off her.

"Well, you sure better hope they have something.

I'm going to keep looking for you, though, baby. Don't make no sense the way folk be out here moving. Just sad," she grumbled.

Saleem flexed his jaw. It was one thing for him to have been out of touch with her and not knowing her needs, but hearing that someone, a man at that, had wronged her had him seeing red.

"If you need—"

"I don't!" Amira snapped, cutting him off. Noticing his nostrils flare, she took the bite out of her tone and said, "Thanks, though."

Saleem licked his lips and nodded. "Yeah... no problem."

Minced words to save her feelings had returned. He retreated to the back, planning to be out of there within thirty minutes. Rekindling things at the moment didn't seem like the move.

Huffing, Amira sat back in her chair. "Mrs. Peterson, you didn't have to bring that up with him in here."

"I didn't mean any harm. But what's the issue with him wanting to help you out? That's the problem with folks today. Especially us Black women. That man wasn't trying to do anything but what a man is supposed to do. Accept the help, baby, and stop stressing yourself out."

Joyce gathered her quicker than an illegal seller on Canal Street when the police pulled up to do a sweep. Amira had nothing to say, so she didn't. Instead, she tidied up her area and gathered her things to head home. She told Joyce she'd be by next week and opened the front door. Her hand paused on the knob, wondering if she should say goodbye to Saleem. Before she could make her decision, he walked down the hallway.

He eyed the bag and purse in her hand. "Still running, huh?"

Amira chuckled. "You know what... have a good night, Saleem."

He smirked, watching her walk out the door, thinking she was done with their conversation and thinking she could keep fucking playing with him. Saleem followed her outside. His long legs made it easy to catch up to her. He caught the car door as she swung it open.

"C'mon, baby. Don't be that way," he said smoothly.

"Why would you say that, of all things?" Amira fussed.

He tilted his head. "Is it not true? You were about to leave and not say a thing to me. That's fucked-up."

Amira squeezed her eyes shut. He was so close to

her face with the door being the only thing between them. "It was nice seeing you."

There. Some honesty. Wasn't that what he wanted?

"Yeah... I know. Can I see you again?"

His question made her shake her head, and Saleem leaned closer, whispering into her ear... in French. *I need to lay eyes on you.* Blushing, Amira held onto the door as the words rolled warmly off his tongue, caressing every crevice of her body. She knew exactly what he'd just told her. Saleem always told her that right before he made a trip to see her. That one sentence offset a tsunami of more emotions for them both.

"Saleem," Amira called his name like she was fed up. They were only beginning... again.

"Angel," he replied, grazing her neck with his lips before standing straight. "You smell so good."

She blew out a deep breath. Saleem wasn't playing fair, and that was the point. Playtime was over.

"Look. I have a lot on my plate right now. I don't think—"

"Don't think then. Shut your brain off for a minute, and let me clear that mothafucka, so there's room for me."

Amira stared at him, unsurprised that he was on her this tough. He always had been. Time and distance meant nothing now that she was in his face. Saleem was feeling too much at once, and whether her return to his life was a blessing or a lesson, he was ready to receive her. Amira needed to get on the same page. He was ready to finish writing their love story.

"Okay," she sighed, a smile inching across her face.

Saleem bit into his juicy bottom lip that she wanted to suck off his face. "See. Was that so hard?"

"Actually, it was. You know me... running and all," she joked.

"Nah. You ain't ran yet," he said seriously, thumbing her chin. Her clit pulsed, reminding her of just how dominantly nasty he was. Saleem kissed her cheek. "I'll be in touch, Angel. Get in the car."

"But... wait. What?" she asked with alarm as he switched up.

"You said okay, and now I'm about to go in the house. Don't you need to get home?"

Confused, wondering what the hell she needed to go home for now, Amira rubbed her eyebrow. "I mean, yeah, sure. Home. That's where I need to go."

Chuckling, Saleem bobbed his head forward. "A'ight. Get in."

Begrudgingly, as she slid into the driver's seat, a pout settled on her face. He did all that just to send her home, and Amira was hot.

"Close my door, please," she sassed, and he chortled.

"How you mad when you were about to leave without saying bye? Fix your face."

Amira playfully rolled her eyes. The chemistry was still there, and there were seemingly no hard feelings—just confused, lustful ones lingering. Looking up at him, Amira smiled brightly.

"Face fixed," she said.

Saleem placed a hand over his chest. "You're fucking beautiful. I swear. Even when you're pouting."

She covered her blush. "Thank you. So, you'll be in touch?"

He nodded. "Yeah."

"But you don't have my number," she said and then laughed. "Never mind."

"Exactly. You changed your number, but I still pay the phone bill every month."

She laughed harder. He wasn't complaining, just stating the obvious. She'd been on his plan since her mama kicked her off hers. If he wanted to reach her, it wasn't hard to do. Saleem had only let her make it this long because he loved her. So, if being out of her life was what she wanted, he abided by her rules.

Back then, he cooperated.

Now, he had no understanding of the feelings she was trying to fight.

Amira may have been the one who got away before, but she wouldn't again. Saleem bet his life on that.

"YOU CAN STILL TELL ME NO, BUT YOU KNOW THE RULES."

FOUR

Amira sat across from the Lincoln family in the small conference room, feeling every bit of their stress. The trio's lives as they once knew it was gone, and getting acclimated to their new temporary normal was necessary. Adjusting the pen in her hand, Amira glanced at the notes she'd taken during their meeting. As their case manager, she wanted to ensure everything was covered.

Mrs. Lincoln's nervous, persistent tapping of her acrylic index nail was appreciated in the otherwise quiet moment. Her husband, Mr. Lincoln, sat beside her, rubbing her back comfortably. Their teenage daughter, True, had her eyes glued to the table's edge like she was counting every scratch on the wood.

"Okay," Amira began, her voice calm and steady. "We covered a lot today, so I'll do a quick recap to make sure everything's clear."

Mr. Lincoln nodded, exhaling like he'd been holding his breath. "That'd be good. I'm trying to keep up with all the new information."

Amira gave him a reassuring smile. "Of course. First, we're locking in those in-home physical therapy sessions for Mrs. Lincoln. The therapist we assigned, Solai, specializes in stroke recovery and comes highly recommended. She'll come out three times a week and work with your doctor to track your progress."

"And her information will be in the paperwork?" Mrs. Lincoln asked.

"Yes. Everything you need will be in this folder," she said, tapping the glossy black folder. "I'll also send an email to the one you listed with contacts."

Mrs. Lincoln nodded. "Thank you. I'm ready to get back to moving like myself again."

"You will," Amira told her confidently. "It isn't going to happen overnight, but every step forward is progress. As long as you stay consistent and keep the faith."

The couple nodded and clasped hands. While her job sometimes involved carrying her work home, Amira wouldn't trade it for anything. She was passionate about helping families and individuals navigate their healthcare journey. It wasn't about titles or paychecks. It was about making sure people felt seen, supported, and knowing that they were capable of pushing through tough times. They didn't last forever.

Amira turned her attention to True. She was only fourteen and struggling with the scare her mother had given them. Navigating feelings and taking on bigger responsibilities around the house was tough, but she was doing it.

"True, I know you're helping a lot at home. It's a lot to take on for anyone, especially someone your age. I want you and your parents to look into this support group for teens who are caregivers. I think you'll enjoy it."

True glanced up, surprised. "Wait. There's a group for kids my age?"

Nodding, Amira said, "Yes. It's a space where you can talk to other teenagers and kids going through the same thing with their families. No judgment."

True's eyes watered. "I'd like that. Thank you so much."

Amira's heart melted. "You're more than welcome. I'll send the details over and have our receptionist gather you a packet. Does that sound good?"

"Yes," True said, nodding. She glanced at her parents with hope in her eyes.

This was why Amira did what she did.

Mrs. Lincoln's lips curved into a small smile as she reached over to squeeze her daughter's hand. "Thank you for thinking of her. That means a lot."

"Of course," Amira said sweetly, like second nature. "Last thing... I've already put in a request for more home care hours through your insurance. It'll probably take a week or two to process, but I'll stay on top of it and let you know if there's any holdup or issues."

Grateful, Mr. Lincoln shook his head as if stunned that she had thought of everything. "You've just got it all covered, huh? I don't know how we would've managed all of this on our own."

Amira smiled. "That's why I'm here. Do you have any questions or concerns before you go?"

He and Mrs. Lincoln shook their heads, standing from their seats. "Not at the moment, but if we do, we'll be sure to reach out," Mr. Lincoln said.

"Please do," Amira said, standing. She gathered the papers into a neat stack, placed them inside the care plan folder, and handed them to Mrs. Lincoln.

"My number is on the bottom of the top page. If anything changes or you all need me, don't hesitate to call."

"We won't," Mrs. Lincoln said. "Thank you so much."

They exited her office in a better mood and more optimistic than they'd entered it, and that's all Amira wanted. Exhaling a small sigh, she glanced at the clock and silently thanked God that her last meeting for the day had been rescheduled. She was heading home early.

After checking a few emails and making sure her schedule for the rest of the week aligned with what she had going on, Amira locked up her office. Thankfully, she was off tomorrow. Stepping outside, she sucked her teeth in annoyance. Instead of it feeling and looking like four in the afternoon, it was damn near pitch black, like it was midnight.

"Seriously, who are they saving the sunlight for? We need it," she grumbled, climbing inside her car.

As her car warmed up, she rolled away the tension in her shoulders and exhaled deeply. Between packing, cleaning, and lifting things, she needed a massage, pronto. One for her feet as well. Her favorite R&B playlist crooned through the speakers as she whipped out of the parking lot. Of course, traffic was a nightmare heading home. It always was at this time of the day.

When she finally arrived twenty-six minutes later, she pulled into the garage and sat there awhile. Decompressing in her car had always been needed after work. Hell, after most days, recently. Knowing the mess she was about to walk into prolonged her relaxation time, too. Amira couldn't function in chaos. So, the disarray of her home was crippling, but she had to go inside.

Closing the garage door, she stepped inside the house and exhaled. She kicked off her booties and slid into her house shoes while eyeing the cluster of boxes, a counter full of things that didn't belong on a counter or in the kitchen, and shit just everywhere. It made her head spin.

"No use in complaining," she mumbled, pulling the door open to her mini wine cellar.

She cracked open a new bottle of Divine, pouring a healthy amount of the semi-sweet red wine into a gold-trimmed goblet. Leaning against the counter, she sipped. She swirled the blend of ripe cherries, subtle spice, and a hint of chocolate in her mouth, humming in appreciation. Then, she got to work. Tired or not, she was on a deadline and would really have to take it there with Mr. Fletcher if he caused more drama about her not being out on time.

Snapping her fingers, Amira reached for another glass plate to wrap. *"Day and night...I know what to do. You're always on my mind, dreaming of you,"* she sang the '02 melody by ISYSS. She kept the four-women-group's album in rotation like it was released yesterday.

Chuckling, she recalled belting the lyrics about being single for the rest of her life from the top of her ten-year-old lungs. Amira took her young, unbroken heart and pink MP3 player through it. Now, she was wondering if she may have spoken those lyrics into existence.

Pausing what she was doing, her mind drifted to Saleem and how he'd yet to get in touch with her. It'd been four days, and she hadn't heard a peep from him. Amira wanted to feel slighted, but she didn't. She chucked it up as him getting his payback for her breaking his heart. Before she could get too deep into her feelings, the music stopped.

The ringing of her phone paused the music floating from her Bluetooth speaker. Recalling where she'd left it, she left the kitchen and walked into the living room, where it sat on the couch. The screen lit up with her mother's name, and Amira sighed so hard. She wasn't in the mood to talk to her but swiped her finger across the screen, anyway, bracing herself.

"Hey, Ma," she said, trying to sound normal.

"Well, hey to you, too. I'm shocked you answered," Evelyn teased. "I thought I was going to get sent to voicemail like last time."

Amira sighed. "I didn't ignore you on purpose. My phone was on two percent."

There was no use in trying to explain that to her.

"Mhm. What are you doing? You sound tired," Evelyn said, her observation laced with a side of judgment.

Amira rubbed her temple and sat on the couch. "I'm packing."

"Oh. Where you headed? You have enough vacation hours?"

The question would have sounded harmless to anyone not privy to their relationship. They'd see it as a mother ensuring her daughter didn't screw up her last paycheck of the year. That wasn't the case for them. Evelyn was questioning her financial status, which made Amira hesitant to let her know why she was tired and packing.

"No. I'm packing to move, Ma," Amira shared.

"Well, that's new. Has it been that long since we've talked?"

Amira rolled her eyes and scoffed, saying, "Months."

"Really?" Evelyn had the nerve to chuckle. "That's... well, I guess that's nothing new. So, where are you moving to?"

Had Amira decided to change her number one day and never posted on social media or talked to other family members, Evelyn wouldn't have known she was alive. She didn't know her daughter, and some days, Amira questioned if she even loved her. That was no exaggeration. Their relationship became strained and almost nonexistent when she went to college.

"Do you care, or are you just doing your monthly call to ease some of the guilt you carry?" Amira questioned, ready to hang up.

Evelyn gasped dramatically for no reason. The theatrical effects long ago stopped working in her favor.

"Of course, I care. Why would I not care about where my daughter is resting her head?"

Amira chuckled. "Okay, Ma. Well, if you must know, I'm moving because my landlord decided to put me out. So, I have a few weeks to pack a home

I've lived in for almost four years and relocate. Still care?"

Sarcasm dripped heavily, oozing through the receiver. Amira didn't know why she expected empathy from her. She said exactly and did what Amira knew she'd do; blame her.

"Did you not pay your rent?"

"Yes, I paid my rent!" Amira snapped, standing up. "I'm not an irresponsible adult who can't—" She stopped her rant before it could fully begin.

There was no use in explaining the situation. Chris, who was still blocked, and Evelyn were one and the same. Not good for a damn thing.

"Well, what are you going to do? The housing market isn't too bad right now. I'm sure you can find something quickly. Hmm. Two weeks. Wow."

Amira put her on speaker and went back to wrapping her glassware. "Yes, wow. That's all you have to say?"

Evelyn clicked her tongue. "I'd offer you a room here, but I'd have to clean it out, and I know you have a ton of things. You wouldn't be so stressed if you had saved up for emergencies like this instead of spending money on trips and those fancy, overpriced dinners you're always posting."

Amira clenched her jaw. Her patience was out

the window. "It's not about me saving. I budget and have the funds to move. It's an inconvenience and something out of my control, but you wouldn't understand that. Everything in your life flows so perfectly, and nothing goes wrong!" Amira spat.

"I never said that. You have to know when to stop making life harder than it has to be," Evelyn said, her tone dripping in supremacy.

Amira let the silence stretch for a moment, biting her tongue. She wanted to call her out of her name so badly that her throat ached.

"Yeah... sure. I'll figure it out."

"You sure better, and I know you will. You always do."

Amira blew out a deep breath. "Was that all you wanted?"

"Yeah. I didn't want much, but this was a good chat. Let me know if you find something. I can't just have you moving into any ol' place."

Amira's eyes rolled *hard* as angry tears filled them. "Right," she choked out.

"Well, talk to you later," Evelyn said, all bubbly as she hadn't just ruined Amira's entire evening.

The call disconnected, and the music resumed. Quickly, Amira paused it. She wasn't in the mood to hear shit. Evelyn calling to do her monthly check-up wasn't anything new. Amira was used to her calls. Today had upset her the most, though. Evelyn was a realtor, one of the best in the city. Yet her daughter couldn't and never would call her for help.

Evelyn always had a way of making Amira feel ten times worse about everything. At first, she didn't understand her behavior, but life had matured her. It opened her eyes and allowed her to witness other people's relationships with their parents. Amira concluded that parental envy was real and that Evelyn could've been the walking billboard for it.

She couldn't fathom that she slept with and got pregnant by a man whom she thought would settle down with her. When he told Evelyn he wanted nothing to do with her or the "mistake" they made, she spiraled. Unintentionally, she treated Amira like the mistake her missing sperm donor told Evelyn she was.

It hurt Amira to her core. Gutted her every time she saw a mother and daughter out bonding when hers wouldn't give her the time of day. She couldn't give two fucks about the man who played a role in her existence. Her mother, though? That was a different type of pain Amira had been trying to soothe in therapy for years. Her therapist was going to have to work overtime during their next session.

Amira thought she was okay with their dynamic, letting it be just who her mother was, but she wasn't. She'd always given her grace when she didn't deserve it. Evelyn tried masking her actions and words as tough love, but there shouldn't be anything tough about a mother's love. It should've been the foundation to nurture, be comforting, selfless, healing, and without conditions or judgment. It's not something that's earned or tested to see how much of it a child deserves.

Years ago, Amira stopped seeing Evelyn as a parent but as a person—one who hadn't healed from her past trauma and projected. Some days, she hoped that her views of her would change, but they hadn't. After today, Amira no longer wanted to keep the line of communication open between them. She just wanted to keep her distance like Evelyn had done her entire life.

Incessant knocking startled Amira out of her deep sleep. Disoriented, she blinked, staring at the faint sunlight filtering through the windows.

Puzzled, she sat up on the couch, popping the crooks out of her neck. *Why am I not in my bed?* she thought, then looked at the coffee table that answered her question.

A bottle of Teremana stared back at her. When the wine didn't soothe the pain from her mother's harsh words, she took a few shots of tequila to drown the ache. Only it made it ten times worse, considering the pounding of her head.

"What the hell," she mumbled, stumbling as she stood from the couch. "Stop knocking so loud," she hissed, thinking she was hollering.

She glanced at the time on the stove on her way to the door— 8:23 a.m. It was much too early on her day off for someone to need her, especially when she hadn't made any plans. Her oversized T-shirt was twisted at the hem, and her silk scarf, which she thankfully hadn't forgotten to put on, was sliding off her head. Adjusting both, she wiped the sleep from her eyes, shuffling toward the door.

Peering out the peephole, Amira's breath hitched, and her brows dented. *"What is he doing here?"* she thought, taking in Saleem's presence. After not hearing from him, she figured he'd decided that they were better off apart. And now, he was standing at her door like it was the most natural thing for him to do. She hesitated with the idea of pretending she wasn't home for all of two seconds. Knowing the man Saleem was, he wasn't about to just walk away.

With a resigned sigh, she unlocked the door and pulled it open. Beaming rays made her shield her squinted eyes before Saleem faced her, obstructing her view. This one was *much* better.

"Good morning, Angel."

Saleem's velvety rasp and his smile woke her right on up. The sun amplified the natural glow of his brown skin and made Amira get lost in his penny-colored eyes. Saleem knew he was fine. The dangerously handsome kind of fine that makes a room pause and women's pulse tick. The type of fine that could pop up at her crib, looking like midnight dipped in finesse, toting an abundance of superb dick and never-ending pockets to match.

He looked too good in a black leather jacket, black tee, and black jeans. The gold chain around his neck was a subtle flex that set the ensemble off. But the jewelry wasn't why Amira was gawking at him. The burnt orange turban wrapped around his head had her stuck. Braids with a black rubber band at the ends were pulled to the back, making her wonder whose hands had been in his head. Amira snapped out of her trance when movement behind him caught her eye. She peeked around him, spotting a moving truck with *JG Movers* scripted across the back.

"Um," she said, clearing her throat. "Good morning. What is all this?"

She gestured at the truck and men unloading dollies and packing supplies.

"Movers," Saleem answered as if it were obvious.

She scratched her scalp. "Huh?"

"They're movers, baby." Saleem chuckled. The expression on her face was cute and comical. "While I take you to breakfast, they'll be here packing your crib up."

Amira blinked, stunned by the lengths he was going to make her fall back in love. That had to be his mission, and he was passing it like a level on GTA.

"Can I come in?" Saleem asked.

Amira stepped to the side, letting him enter. Her eyes widened when he wrapped her in a hug and kissed her cheek.

As quickly as he embraced her, Saleem let her go and asked, "How'd you sleep?"

Thrown off, Amira wondered if she was even awake. All of this felt like a dream. "Like a baby." She chuckled. "You?"

Saleem eyed her bare thighs. Her shorts were barely visible, thanks to their length and her T-shirt. He slept wonderfully, knowing that when he woke up this morning, her place was his first stop.

"I slept, a'ight. I'm a lil' hungry, though. You ate?"

"I haven't even brushed my teeth," Amira said, laughing.

Saleem smirked. "That's what that smell is?"

"Oh, whatever. You weren't complaining when you just hugged me and kissed my cheek."

"No reason to complain when I'm trying to keep it respectful by not sticking my tongue down your throat. *That's* how you should've been greeted. Be grateful I have some restraint, Angel."

His admission shut Amira up and made her pussy talk. *Girl, what are we doing?!*

"Right...okay. Be grateful," Amira mumbled, flustered out of her mind. Her nipples were so hard, she knew he could spot them through her shirt.

"Thank you," Saleem teased. "Now, can I take you to breakfast or do you have other plans this morning?"

"You ask this after you pull up to my home with strangers?" she questioned.

"They're not strangers. I know them."

She chuckled. "Of course, you do. You're not going to take no for an answer, are you?"

He could've. He'd lived this long hearing the word no. It just made him go harder.

"I wouldn't like to, but you can tell me no under one condition," Saleem said.

Amira's expression urged him to explain. "Mhm, and what is that?"

"If you can tell me in French that you'd rather not have breakfast with me and pack this house up on your own, I'll leave you alone."

Her eyes widened, and mouth dropped. "You *know* I can't say all of that in French. That's not fair!"

"And neither is the way my stomach is touching my back, baby." Saleem chuckled. "I'll wait down here and let my people in while you get dressed. Anything you don't want them to pack up?"

Saleem took it upon himself to make Amira's life easier. He knew she'd never ask, especially considering their circumstances, and she didn't give him a chance to offer any assistance. That was cool with Saleem. He'd always been a man of action anyway. A true leader like he was raised to be—all mothafucking man.

Amira's throat ached with bubbling emotions as she stared at him. She'd spent the night crying because she was stressed, tipsy, and exhausted from juggling life. It was smacking her upside the head, and here Saleem came to save the day.

When her eyes misted, Saleem's nostrils flared. "Don't do that. Seeing you cry gon' make me ruin a lot of people's day."

She didn't mean to chuckle, but he was funny. Funny but dead serious because she knew he meant it. "I'm not sad. I mean, I was."

"Because you have to move?"

"No," she said, shaking her head. "I've come to terms with that. I talked to my mama last night and..." She swallowed her tears down.

Saleem knew their history. He never liked Evelyn and hated the way she treated Amira. Even though they weren't together, he always wondered if they mended their relationship. Seeing her upset answered his question. He waited for her to gather herself.

"And she only made things worse. Didn't offer me any type of help, and then you show up wanting me to readily agree to everything you're offering me. I...I'm just not used to this."

Nodding, Saleem said, "You're not used to it anymore, and I blame myself for that."

"No. Don't say that. Don't do that." She shook her head vehemently.

"It's the truth. As for your mother... no disrespect, but she made you hyper-independent, Angel. She left you no choice but to fend for yourself and looked at it as you not needing her or anyone else."

Amira hiccupped, slightly tasting the shots from hours prior. "It's fine."

"No, it's not." Saleem's tone was soft but firm. "You're exhausted from trying to do it all."

"What other choice do I have? Hmm? I get things done because I know I can."

"I'm your choice. Use me. Depend on me because whether we're together or not, I got you."

Amira shook her head, and her chest tightened at his words. She looked away, blinking rapidly. Gratitude filled her heart, and Saleem filled the space between them. He didn't reach out and hold her like he wanted to do, remembering the restraint he spoke of. Had he, they wouldn't be leaving her crib, and the movers wouldn't be packing a damn thing.

Instead, he swiped the tears on her cheeks and said, "This time, I'm not taking no for an answer. No, you can't push me away or stop me from taking care of you. Stop trying. Hang up the thought of me rejecting you and doing some lame shit, 'cause I know that's what's running through that pretty lil' head of yours."

Amira inhaled a stuttered breath. "My head is little?"

Saleem chuckled. "It got a little bigger," he jested, loving the smile she gave him.

Her heart thudded happily in her chest, and for once, she didn't have a snappy comeback. Instead, Amira cleared her throat and told him what he wanted to hear.

"No more saying no," she said, feeling crazy for even uttering the words.

"Nah, you can still tell me no, but you know the rules."

She rolled her eyes playfully. "Well, I'm fucked."

Smirking, Saleem backpedaled away from her. *How the hell does he make walking backward attractive?* Amira thought and licked her lips.

"I can't wait to hear you say yes for the rest of our lives," he said.

"Now, you're taking it too far." Amira laughed as he opened the door.

Little did she know, Saleem hadn't taken it far at all. Not yet.

"I WAS JUST FINISHING WHAT YOU STARTED."

FIVE

"Do you still like your coffee straight black and a little sweet?" Amira asked, her head tilted as she studied Saleem with a hint of curiosity.

She had a lot of questions and was grateful they were seated at a booth in the corner where there was minimal foot traffic. Lotus, the brunch spot he brought her to, had a laid-back vibe and some of the best buttermilk pancakes in the city. Amira loved a crispy-edge waffle, but she'd switch it up sometimes.

Saleem blinked, momentarily lost in all of her. They almost didn't leave the house once Amira was dressed. She hadn't put on anything over the top, just a black silk button-down that she tied at the front and tucked, her favorite American Eagle jeans, and a comfortable heel. Her hair was straightened, framing her face in the coldest layers, thanks to her stylist, Moo.

She was so effortlessly gorgeous that Saleem was thrown off his square. His heart did this stupid little flutter, skipping a beat when his eyes landed on her lips. Those pretty soft lips that once whispered promises and screams with his name attached as he made love to her. Amira had gotten lucky this morning. When she waved a hand in his face, he snapped out of it.

"My fault, baby. What'd you say?" he asked.

Smirking, Amira laced her fingers together. "I asked if you still drank your coffee the same. You're not paying me no mind," she assumed.

"I'm giving you all my attention; that's how I missed your question," he said. His voice was low and smooth.

Amira blushed. "Tell me anything."

"Nah. I'm serious," he countered. "You've been walking around this whole time single and looking like—" He paused, shaking his head as his lips quirked in a small smile. *Looking like I should put a boulder on your finger and a few babies in your belly.* His thoughts were immediate. Their future flashed before his eyes like a snapshot of a picture.

"Looking like what?" Amira questioned, humored by his actions.

"I don't even know. You made me forget what I was going to say."

Chuckling, Amira said, "That's payback for what you said earlier. You really wanted to stick your tongue down my throat?" she teased.

Saleem shook his head. "No. I had other places in mind... but I can start there. Finish where I *know* it's real warm and sticky."

His molten gaze had Amira tossing her hair off her neck. She wanted to fan herself.

"Saleem," she breathed out.

"You took it there," he said, then thanked the waiter for dropping their drinks off before he confirmed that their food would be out shortly.

The peppermint tea Saleem added one sugar to was piping hot, while the Sprite Amira ordered cooled her hot ass off with a few sips. She hoped it helped ease the queasiness of her stomach, thanks to Saleem and that damn tequila. Although his week-long fast ended a few days ago, Saleem was still eating light. He ordered a side of fruit, shrimp and grits with scrambled eggs and toast, while Amira opted for a waffle, veggie omelet with light cheese, and sausage links.

"I was just finishing what you started," she said, shrugging when the waiter walked off.

"Yeah... okay, Angel. To answer your question, yes. I still like my coffee black. One or two sugars. I'm more into herbal teas now, though."

"Nooow," she dragged, making him shake his head, already knowing where she was going with it. "It took you what... ten years to transition?"

"A few weeks," he answered.

Saleem wasn't going to tell her how he'd been so sick from their breakup that he went out and bought all the teas she used to try and make him drink when they were together. His grandma hadn't even been able to do that unless he was forced. He went the extra mile just to feel like he was close to her.

"Oh," Amira chirped, wondering who converted his addiction. "Well, that's good for you. I know Jennie Mae would be proud. I am," she said sincerely.

Her words meant more than she said and held more weight than she knew.

Saleem pulled his bottom lip into his mouth. "She would be. Thank you. I'm proud of you, too. You got that degree like you said you would."

She wiggled her index and middle finger. "Two degrees."

"I'm not surprised. Tell me something I don't know. What is it like in my Angel's world?"

She arched an eyebrow, caught off guard by his question and how he'd asked it. "What's it like?"

"Yeah. Give me a glimpse. What... you don't yap people's ears off anymore?" he asked, joking with her.

She laughed. Amira was a certified yapper when they were together. Long-distance did that to her, but honestly, they could talk about anything and nothing at all. That was the beauty of what they shared, like this morning. Amira had openly expressed her feelings, and instead of Saleem shutting them down, he embraced them without judgment; just sound advice and a resolution for her troubles.

Saleem wanted to experience everything about Amira; observe her in a new light that wasn't dimmed by the world's misfortunes and people who didn't deserve her energy.

She laughed. "I do."

"A'ight. Talk to me then," Saleem urged.

"I don't really do much." She shrugged, thinking. "I try to start my mornings with a nice stretch. Yes, don't look like that."

Saleem smirked. "You used to hate when I'd call and wake you up on my way to the gym."

While Saleem used to start his morning by driving to the gym, Amira would snuggle under her covers until he got there. They stretched together over the phone, and then he worked out while she prepared for class. The long-distance thing hadn't been an issue until it was.

"It stuck with me, I guess." She shrugged like it was nothing. That meant everything to him. To her, too. It was little reminders of what they shared.

"It's a good habit to have. What you be doing after work?"

"Depends on the day," she said as their food was brought out.

Her eyes lit up, and her stomach rumbled at the aromas. Going inside her purse, Amira squirted some hand sanitizer into her palm before giving Saleem some. Once he rubbed it in, he reached for Amira's hand, holding it. Her eyes shot up to him, but his head was already bowed.

"Heavenly Father, we thank you for this meal and the hands that prepared it. Bless this food to nourish our bodies, strengthen our hearts, and sharpen our minds. We praise you for your endless mercy and provision. In Jesus' name and by your will, Amen."

"Amen," Amira said.

Hearing him pray brought a feeling of peace over her like no other. The nostalgia couldn't be explained. While she was stuck, remembering all the times they'd prayed together and the times he'd prayed over her, Saleem was focused on his plate.

"You want a strawberry?" he asked, extending his fork that pierced through the fruit.

Amira didn't even know why he asked if he was going to feed her anyway. She nodded, accepting the sweet red berry, and chewed slowly. Saleem was acting as if this was their normal; breakfast dates on chilly mornings before running errands and returning home to relax. It was scary, and Amira shook her head to weed away the negative thoughts trying to creep in.

"Good?" he asked.

She nodded. "Mhm. What's wrong?" she asked, seeing him frown at his plate.

"They put cheese on my eggs. It's coo', though."

"No, it's not," Amira said, body pivoting and eyes roaming to find their water. "You don't like cheese on your eggs. You would've asked for that if that's what you wanted."

"Baby, it's fine. It's not that—"

Amira waved him off. "Be quiet, Saleem. Excuse me," she said, grabbing their waiter's attention.

"Yes. How did everything come out?"

"Wrong," Amira said sharply, reaching across the table for Saleem's plate. "There wasn't supposed to be cheese on his eggs."

Visibly shaken by her tone and the kitchen's mistake, the waiter said, "I'm so sorry about that. I'll have the kitchen remake them."

"With fresh toast as well," she stated.

"Of course. I'll have that right out for you."

He walked off, and Amira sat back in her seat. Saleem's eyes sparkled with pure love as she sipped her Sprite like she hadn't damn near bit the man's head off.

"Now, what were you saying?" she asked, and Saleem cracked up.

"Aye. You're something else."

She shrugged. "Whatever. You were just going to eat those damn eggs and not speak up for yourself. Grow up," she teased, laughing.

"Man, watch out," he chortled. "Thank you, though. My stomach would've been messed up for the rest of the day."

"Mhm. You're welcome."

They ate in silence once Saleem's correct order was brought out. Amira devoured her waffle, the warm syrup making it even more enjoyable. While she ate and danced in her seat, Saleem's eyes found her every few seconds. Perfection. That's what she was in his eyes, and he couldn't seem to understand where they, where he, had gone wrong. Their mornings should've been spent like this.

A few mini-mes sitting beside us. His thoughts always went there.

"You want some?" Amira asked, watching him watch her.

Saleem looked at her almost-gone waffle, then her glossy lips as she licked a drop of syrup off. She had no idea what the innocent action did to the fabric of his jeans.

"Nah, I'm good. I'm glad you enjoying it, though."

She smiled. It was more than just the meal that had her grinning. Sitting her fork down, she sipped some of her water. Amira rested her chin in her palm, smiling with curiosity as she studied him.

"How are your siblings?" she asked.

Saleem leaned back in his chair, a faint smile tugging at his lips. "My siblings are good. Grown as hell and still giving me the blues."

"Which is warranted as the oldest," she teased.

"Tayah and Yuhani are gorgeous. It makes sense that one of them got into modeling."

Saleem nodded. "Yeah. Tay loves that shit. She tried to get Nini into it, but she loves doing hair."

"Runs in the family." Amira grinned, remembering how he used to complain about how heavy-handed Tiffany was.

"True," Saleem agreed.

"And your brother?"

Saleem's expression shifted. A mix of amusement and exasperation marred his features. "Rahim be on go all the time. Always finding something new to get into." His answer was cryptic, protecting his brother's sporadic image and personality.

"That's okay. The world needs people like him," Amira said, remembering what it was like trying to find her footing in life at twenty-five. She was still misplacing it at thirty-two. Rahim would be just fine.

"I feel you. How's your brother? He's in college, right?"

Her answer stalled. "Um...yeah. Drew is in college."

Amira wanted to ask him how he even knew that. Drew was seven when she met Saleem. He was twenty now, in college, and had just texted Amira while she was getting dressed. He'd been courteous enough to ask if he could send her his Christmas list. She felt terrible because gifts were the last thing on her mind.

Saleem asking about him magnified the number of years they'd been apart. More than anything, it highlighted how he'd been keeping count, too.

"That's what's up. I guess we didn't do too bad," he said, knowing their role as the oldest child mimicked being a parent.

Amira agreed. Drew was away at her alma mater, passing every course as a college athlete. If his education didn't land him a good job, shooting hoops would. Amira knew that for a fact.

"I guess not," she said.

Amira watched him gather their dishes, making their waiter's job easier by stacking them neatly. His selfless actions had always been commendable. He'd always been thoughtful, but this version of him felt...steady. It was like she was seeing a side of him that she hadn't fully appreciated before.

Saleem's every move and every word he spoke were with masculine poise. Amira loved that he was assertive but not overbearing. He knew how to lead without diminishing others, a quiet power few men possessed. Saleem made people naturally respect him and feel secure in his presence, and Amira was happy to be one of those people.

When he finished, he wiped his hands with a wet wipe and leaned against the cushioned seat. "I wanted to talk to you about something, and just hear me out, a'ight?" He added the last part once he saw her squint.

"Okay. What is it?"

"I have a place you can move into."

She opened her mouth to argue but closed it just as quickly when he shook his head.

"You remember the rules, right?" Saleem asked, and she playfully rolled her eyes.

"Remind me to resume French lessons."

"That'll be your best bet." He smirked, then got serious. "Those movers aren't at your crib for no reason. I was going to leave it alone." He paused when she raised a brow, silently calling his bluff. He laughed. "A'ight. I wasn't going to leave it alone. You know me."

Do I? is what she wanted to ask, but she didn't want to ruin the mood. Saleem elaborated, sensing that she needed a bit more convincing.

"I wasn't feeling your situation or the predicament you were in. So, I'm offering you a place. It might be a little too big, but you can grow into it," Saleem said.

He was talking as if she'd already accepted his offer. As if the plan was to be there beyond the standard length of a leasing period. Amira didn't want to say no but didn't feel inclined to say yes. After all, she had broken his heart. Saleem didn't owe her anything, but she had to know one thing. Nothing in life was for free, even if it didn't cost money.

"And if I accept this house, what do you expect from me in return?"

"I want you to be my wife."

"I PROMISE YOU I WON'T BE AS ACCOMMODATING."

SIX

Saleem was out of his mind.

That's the only conclusion Amira could come up with as the absurd request fell from his lips.

"Your wife?" she repeated, semi-yelling, with her heart pounding and body stiffening.

Saleem wasn't alarmed by her reaction. He was amused and calm. *Too* damn calm as if he knew her answer would be yes. This was...very Amira-coded.

"Yes. My wife. Does that not work for you?"

Considering her circumstances and his, he was hoping it did.

"Do I look like a charity case?" she snarled, arms crossing over her chest.

"No," he said firmly, thankful that he could now tell her what he saw in her from his point of view.

She asked earlier, but he refrained from explaining. Too caught up in their reconnection.

"You look beautiful." Her frown fell. "And like a woman who I intend to help because she should know that as long as I'm on this earth and even when I'm not, she'll never have to break her back or her pockets."

Amira swallowed and, as casually as she could manage, asked, "You're serious?"

"Dead serious."

This was a lot to take in. He'd just popped back into her world and wanted her to be his wife? That wasn't something to toy with or take lightly.

"Saleem. That's... that's not just something you casually ask someone. Marriage isn't—"

"Something I would ever play about. Especially not with you," he cut her off.

Amira let out a disbelieving chuckle. What she wanted in her early twenties was still the same thing she wanted now, but at what cost? Partnership, love, stability, loyalty, devotion, and, most of all, a family wasn't something she ever wanted to settle for out of desperation. *But am I really settling?* she thought, twirling the end of her loc. Saleem focused on her hand and bare ring finger, envisioning what it'd look like once he weighed it down.

"So, I have to settle because I'm homeless?" she asked.

"Settle?" His eyes narrowed with a slight squint. "I wouldn't call that settling when you can get everything you want from me. This ain't about convenience or charity. I'm offering this because I know what I want, and I want you to have the best of everything. I wasn't aware that the definition had changed."

Amira sighed. "This is... I don't know. I know there's more to this." She was a smart woman. A bit difficult, but intelligent, nonetheless. "I'ma need you to explain it to me. You want me to be your wife for what, exactly?"

This was the part Saleem had been waiting on. He'd thrown the proposition at her without warning, so it was only right that he gave her the rundown. Amira listened intently as he broke everything down. Her mind was swirling with questions and doubts.

"So, it's expected of me," Saleem said, wrapping up his spiel, leaving out one key detail.

"And you haven't found any eligible women or am I your last resort?" she asked, chuckling.

"You're my first and only choice."

Saleem didn't crack a grin; didn't mince his

words to save her feelings. He only made her plummet deeper into them.

Her lips parted, but no words came out. His confession was jarring, considering their past. Amira just knew there had been plenty of women he could've asked, but there wasn't. Saleem had no desire to give another woman the opportunity to say he asked for their hand in marriage.

"This is crazy," she said, downing her water. "I mean, I know I'd be doing you a favor, but if you wanted to truly just help me, why not just give me the house?

"You can have it," he said nonchalantly.

"Saleem."

He smirked. "Angel."

"What do you mean I can have it?"

"Take my money. My house and my car. For one hit of you... you can have it all, baby."

Amira smiled so embarrassingly hard, her cheeks heated. The way he just sat there and sang K-Ci's intro to *Feenin'* had her squirming in her seat.

"Want me to keep going? I can do this all day," he said.

She shook her head, laughing. "No. Even though you don't sound half bad, you need to focus on what you're asking of me."

It wasn't that she couldn't find a place to stay or didn't have the funds. It was the principle. Well, before, it was the daunting task of packing, which was no longer an issue.

"I know this isn't ideal, and you're probably over there thinking that I've lost my mind, but—"

"For how long?" Amira asked, cutting his sentence short.

A look of confusion crossed his face, but he quickly fixed it. Saleem knew telling her forever would scare her away and have her running out of the restaurant, so he went with the next best answer. One he hoped she agreed with.

"For however long you want. It has to be more than a year, though," he stated.

Truthfully, he didn't need that much time to make her see that this wasn't out of obligations and circumstantial but because they were meant to be. But he knew her shifty ass needed rules. Amira thought about it. *A year isn't that long. It'll fly by,* she thought.

"And then, we'll call it quits or still fake it?"

He chuckled at the unseriousness of her question. "I won't be faking anything, but yeah. We can do whatever makes you comfortable."

"And if I want a divorce?"

Saleem shook his head and exhaled. After all these years, she was still running. Her mother and aunties had really done a number on her. Back then, college and distance stopped him from being able to chase her. Now? Now, Saleem was on her ass like back pockets. There wouldn't be a divorce if he had any say.

"You won't want one," he said with the utmost confidence.

Amira smirked. "Sure. Do I have time to think about moving in and all?"

Saleem scratched his eyebrow, giving her a weird look. "Not really. You're on a deadline, and I'd prefer we spend time together before my dad returns home in two months."

Her eyes stretch. "Two months?" she whispered, afraid to hear him repeat what she knew he said.

Saleem nodded. "Yes. He's returning earlier than I expected, and my mama already told me I better not piss her husband off with my bullshit."

Shaking her head, Amira reached for her water, quickly realizing she had none left. Saleem slid her his glass, and without thinking, she wrapped her lips around his straw. He wanted to tell her that only couples do shit like that, but instead, he just smirked as she chugged it down.

"Fuck," she grumbled and sighed. That wasn't nearly enough time to mentally prepare to act like someone's wife. A little voice in her head said, *Make it enough*, mimicking Smokey's mama from *Friday*. "Okay. I'll do it," she said, staring him in those spellbinding eyes.

"Yeah?" Saleem tried masking the excitement in his voice.

She nodded. "Mhm. On a few conditions. You aren't the only one with rules around here."

Saleem licked his lips and grinned. "A'ight. Let me hear em'."

"This doesn't mean we're together...like romantically. We're doing each other a favor."

He gave her an impish grin. "Got it."

"And we need boundaries. Clear ones. None of that *we're married, so we have to act like it*, mess. I'm not playing house."

"Technically, you will be."

Her brows pinched. "How's that?"

"We'll be under the same roof."

"But...I..." She paused to think. "You said you had a house for *me*. Not us."

"I do. It's mine and now yours once I add your name to the deed."

She rubbed her forehead. Amira wanted to be

shocked, but she didn't think anything else could surprise her this afternoon. That was until Saleem leaned across the table, dangerously close to her lips. Amira pressed her thighs together, thinking he was about to kiss her.

"Did you think I'd be resting my head somewhere my wife doesn't lay hers?"

Unable to give him a verbal answer, Amira shook her head. Smiling, Saleem kissed her lips. "I'm glad we're on the same page, Angel," he said, then retreated to his side of the table like he hadn't just shifted her world in a way she never saw coming.

Right then, Amira concluded that she would be violating every rule she tried to establish for this arrangement. How could she not?

It wasn't often that Saleem had to revert to his old ways, but certain situations brought out a side of him that wasn't to be played with.

He hadn't been directly violated, but he might as well have been, and someone had to pay. Saleem eyed the tiny, poorly decorated living room with disgust. A gaudy leather couch was being disassembled and carried out, while the sixty-five-inch TV had just been removed from the wall. A faint smell of mildew was in the air, and Saleem couldn't help but wonder how the nigga hadn't gotten whatever the issue was fixed, seeing as though he was a landlord and all.

He didn't care either way because all of this shit was about to be gone. Saleem wasn't here for comfort. He was here to handle business. The clock above the fireplace ticked dauntingly, matching the rhythm of Saleem's steady heartbeat. He'd already peeped the photo frames on the mantel. Mr. Fletcher had a goofy-ass grin on his face that didn't match the energy of a man, who thought he could just toss a woman out on the street. Especially, Amira. Nah, that wasn't going to fly. Not today or any other day if Saleem had any say-so.

"Aye, Boss," a bald-head guy said, stepping through the open front door. "Everything out here is free?"

Saleem nodded. "Yeah. Take whatever."

The man nodded upward. "Bet that. Good looking."

"Thank that bitch ass owner," Saleem said.

Mr. Fletcher would be in for a rude awakening

when he came home. Saleem opted to leave work early and post up at his crib. On the drive over, he thought about making his ass disappear for playing with his baby, but then, he came up with a better idea.

Every few minutes, headlights from cars brightened the living room. He'd hear movement outside, and then the vehicles pulled off. Saleem had thrown Mr. Fletcher a surprise garage sale and he didn't even know it.

It'd been a good two hours of him waiting, and Saleem planned to camp out all night or track his ass down if he didn't hurry up. That wouldn't be the case, though. Thanks to all the yelling he was doing, Saleem heard the exact moment he arrived.

"Nigga better pipe down," he said, straightening his posture on the stool he was sitting on.

Heavy footsteps shuffled into the house, and then the bitch-ass man himself appeared. Mr. Fletcher was in his mid-fifties, balding, and looking just as sour as Saleem had imagined.

"Who the hell are you?" he barked, eyes narrowing as he noticed Saleem's calm but unbothered posture.

Coolly, Saleem lifted the cup of one of his juices he'd been drinking to his mouth. With one foot planted on the ground and the other perched on the stool, he drank it until there was nothing left, staring Mr. Fletcher in the eyes. He slurped loudly, clearing the pineapple peach contents, burped even louder, and then disrespectfully tossed the plastic cup on the ground.

"Normally, I wouldn't litter, but this place is a dump anyway," he said and stood. Saleem smiled, but it didn't reach his eyes as he stepped his way. "You're late. I was starting to think you weren't gonna show."

"Who the hell are you! And what'd you do with all of my things? I'm calling the po—"

Saleem cut his sentence short with a swift punch to the center of his neck. Mr. Fletcher clasped a hand around his neck, further restricting his breathing. Gripping him around the collar of his worn shirt, Saleem yoked him up and walked toward the open door. Without breaking a sweat, Saleem stepped outside and flung him onto the yard.

"Gotdamn! He just threw that man out of his own crib!" someone picking up a dresser yelled.

Mr. Fletcher struggled to stand up as Saleem kneeled beside him. The hand he placed on his shoulder damn near fractured his bone as he squeezed.

"It doesn't feel good to get put out on your ass, does it?"

His eyes watered with pure fear as he coughed out unformed sentences. "She...I. It wasn't—"

Saleem cut him off, his voice low but commanding. "It should've never fucking happened. Trying to put her out was your first mistake." Mr. Fletcher pissed his pants when cold steel pressed against his exposed skin. "The second mistake was threatening her. I'd end your life, but I love hers too much to break her heart and be placed behind bars for some lame."

He pressed the barrel deeper into his skin. "But I will," Saleem said coldly.

Tears rolled down Mr. Fletcher's cheeks. He had no idea who he'd been fucking with. Hopefully, he got the picture now.

"Pl-Please, man," he begged.

"Shut the fuck up, pissy!" Saleem spat. "I expect my wife's security deposit to be pending in her bank account by tomorrow. Any paperwork insinuating that she was evicted no longer exists. Do I make myself clear?"

Mr. Fletcher swallowed hard and nodded.

"Good. If it's not, you'll see me again, and I promise you I won't be as accommodating.

Remember this conversation and think twice before you try to fuck over a woman who has people ready to take your pathetic life on her behalf."

Standing from his squatted position, Saleem tucked his gun and adjusted his black peacoat. He gave Mr. Fletcher one last warning look and walked to his truck. He smiled, passing a few people who had stopped to see what was going on and collect some things from the curb.

"Happy holidays," Saleem said cheerfully.

He was headed home to see his Angel and was in a good mood again.

"LET IT FLOW OR LET IT GO."

SEVEN

Amira stood inside her new walk-in closet, hanging a few of her things up. Thanks to the team of people Saleem hired, she hadn't had to unpack much, but putting away her belongings in a closet the size of a bedroom was so satisfying. Plus, she loved the feel of the velvet hangers. She was already plotting to tear down the mall to fill empty spots and the island dresser in the middle of the floor. Reaching for a pair of jeans that fell, she accidentally dropped her phone.

"Oop. Hello?" she said, hoping it hadn't hung up.

"I'm here," Jazmine said.

Amira placed the phone on the dresser. "Okay. Now, what were you saying?"

"You just gon' act like he ain't do all that?" Jazmine's voice dripped with amusement.

Amira snorted. "Girl, I didn't even know he did anything."

Once most of her belongings had been moved into the house and she kept a few essentials at her place, Mr. Fletcher didn't cross her mind. Especially not when she received her security deposit plus interest before turning her keys in. Amira was confused as to why he added on an extra three hundred dollars, but now she knew why. She stayed at her townhome for a little over a week after their talk at the restaurant. Saleem hadn't exaggerated when he said it may be too big, but it was hers, so she wasn't complaining.

"Mhm. Sure you didn't."

"I'm for real! Can you blame him, though? If you don't knock a man on his ass for disrespecting me, is it real?" Jazmine cracked up on the other end, laughing so loud that Amira had to lower her volume.

"It's not real at all! He made that poor man piss on himself. I'm crying!"

They cackled. Amira didn't even know Saleem had paid the man a visit until her phone blew up with calls a few days later. Someone had recorded the entire thing, and it went viral. Thankfully, Saleem hadn't gotten into any trouble. She didn't want that to smear his image in any way. Little did Amira know, Saleem was looking like a hero. Mr. Fletcher was a horrible landlord, and it was only a matter of time before he showed Amira his true colors.

"What did he say when he came back?" Jazmine asked.

Amira leaned against the dresser, shaking her head but unable to stop the smile spreading across her face. "He didn't say much. Just walked in, gave me a kiss, and was like, 'I handled that lil' pissy problem you had.' Like I requested him to be handled, and we're living out an action movie or something."

Jazmine hollered. "Not *pissy problem*! Please get off my phone. What is wrong with him?"

They couldn't stop laughing.

"Sis, when I say he was in such a good mood, I'm not lying. Just smiling and all."

"Chile, that man is lowkey crazy and nuts about you," Jazmine expressed.

Amira simpered. "You think so?"

"Girl, I know so. I knew that man didn't play about you when he drove four hours just to make you tell him to his face that it was over. Whew! You're stronger than me. I would've caved, Mira."

She caved the following morning. Saleem caught her on her way to the dining hall and asked for a few minutes of her time. She gave him those couple of minutes, but there hadn't been any talking. Saleem's feelings were hurt, so he took it out on her pussy in the back of his car. He ate her out until she was begging for him to stop and fucked her so good, Amira couldn't walk or see straight when he sent her on her way. She limped right back to their dorm, skipped class, and cried herself to sleep.

Jazmine didn't need to know that. They shared an intimate, vulnerable moment, and some memories were better kept private.

"You see what not caving got me," Amira said.

"Yeah. A man who became a shiesty landlord overnight. Out here evicting folks like that."

Amira chuckled as she made her way downstairs. "You're ridiculous. He didn't evict him. Just... readjusted his attitude and living arrangement a little bit."

"A little?" Jazmine deadpanned. "Amira, that man probably can't even sleep at night. Saleem done scared him straight!"

They both sputtered laughter, the sound echoing

through the massive home. Amira shrugged, making it to the kitchen. "Oh well. Fuck him."

"Straight up. But for real," Jazmine said after a beat, her tone softening. "I'm glad y'all reconnected. Had it not been for Mr. Pissy, you wouldn't be up in that nice ass house."

Truthfully, Amira wouldn't be here had she not agreed to marry him. She'd yet to divulge that information to Jazmine, Quinn, or her friends. She didn't want to be stuck looking a fool if things went left and didn't work out. She'd learned over the years that some things were better left unshared, no matter how close she was to someone.

Amira smiled. "I am, too."

"You sound and look happier. I know you had so much going on and tend to overthink, but don't with this, okay? Let it flow or let it go. It's clear you two are meant to be in each other's lives," Jazmine commented, not realizing the weight of her words and how badly Amira needed to hear them.

"Let it flow or let it go," she repeated. "I love that. And you know me. Quick to end something."

Jazmine chuckled. "Exactly. Speaking of ending things... has Evelyn called you again?"

Like Saleem, Jazmine had been a witness over their young adult years of her irrational parenting.

Jazmine overheard so many conversations where she had wanted to snatch the phone up and curse her out, especially when Evelyn would tell Amira that she needed better friends.

She's only saying that because she doesn't think you deserve people in your life who love you, Jaz had said so naturally that it stunned Amira to tears.

It was the truth. She never sugar-coated anything with Amira, so she wouldn't regarding her relationship with her mother. Evelyn was toxic.

"No. You know she goes on these hiatuses from me as if she needs a break." Amira chuckled.

"She needs to stay gone. "If you can block that nigga, Chris, you can block her," Jazmine said.

"I did. I thought I told you that," Amira said, placing her phone on the glossy granite island.

The entire place screamed Saleem's personality, and ironically, it matched the vibe Amira loved. At her age, she didn't think she'd ever have modern, sleek, top-of-the-line appliances. The touchscreen refrigerator was her favorite kitchen feature, second to the seven-burner gas stove with a double oven. The same day Amira agreed to move in, Saleem made a few calls to get the house deep cleaned, furnished, and decorated. He wasn't wasting any time.

"I'm talking about for good, Amira, on everything. From everything. This new life you're embarking upon doesn't deserve to be interrupted by toxicity. I know the second you answer her calls or see anything related to her, you're in a foul mood. I hate that, and I love you too much to watch you still give her access to any part of you."

Amira thought she was done crying for the month. It was a new year, and she'd already cried twice. Though happy tears at first, Jazmine was making the waterworks return. She sniffled, dabbing underneath her eyes where tears had gathered but hadn't fallen.

"So, go completely no contact?" Amira proposed, leaning against the counter.

"It wouldn't be the first time, but for the best."

Amira sighed. She'd discussed this with her therapist but hadn't made the decision yet. A part of her knew that once she really enforced her boundaries, their relationship would be completely over. But, after the stunt she pulled when Amira needed her the most, it wasn't the worst idea.

"You're right," Amira said.

"And listen... I know you love her. Going no-contact doesn't mean you have to stop. It just means you love and choose to prioritize yourself more. If someone has an issue with that, tell them to come see me."

Amira chuckled. "You sound like my—" She caught herself.

Thankfully, Jazmine caught on, giving Saleem a title that didn't begin with the letter H like Amira was about to do. *Relax, girl. Y'all aren't even married yet*, she said to herself.

"Your man?" Jazmine laughed and clapped. "I know that's fucking right. Let me find out he over there dicking you down and making you get your act together."

Playfully, Amira rolled her eyes and grabbed a knife from the drawer. "Getting my act together is crazy."

"No, what was crazy was breaking up with that man, but I'ma leave the past in the past." Jazmine snickered.

"Why, thank you. How kind of you to leave me be."

They laughed, and Amira's stomach growled so loud that Jazmine quieted.

"Was that...I know that was not your stomach. Is he over there starving you? Oh, my gosh."

Leaning over the counter, Amira's body bounced

with laughter. "Jaz, please shut the hell up! Why would that man not be feeding me?"

"I don't know, hell! You be talking about how he stops eating meat every month or some shit. You might be doing the same thing."

When Amira didn't say anything, confirming her friend's suspicions, Jazmine hollered.

"What has he done to you!" she cried dramatically.

Amira wanted to see if fasting from meat would increase her energy and give her more mental clarity. That was it.

"You have no sense." Amira laughed and then coughed into the crook of her arm. She could hardly breathe.

"And you ain't gon' have no ass if you keep on. This is ridiculous," she teased, laughing.

"He's always been healthy; that's nothing new. If anything, he's around here getting me thicker with all the food he's been cooking and having me taste."

Trying to stick to her word and not cross the line with Saleem, Amira had slept at her townhome until she got word that her bedroom furniture for their new home would be delivered. Unfortunately for her, with it being her first day staying at the house, the delivery company had to reschedule due to inclement weather.

Amira kept up her end of the deal and spent time with him as he'd asked, but she was trying to avoid sleeping under the same roof as him. She'd get off work, see what he was doing, and he'd either go see her, or she'd spend the evening at his place before going to her townhome. Now, she couldn't run. Time was up.

"Ah. What a life." Jazmine hummed, happy for her girl. "All Keenan knows how to make is spicy gourmet Nongshim noodles and put chicken in the air fryer."

Amira chuckled and defended Keenan. "And you eat both, so hush."

"And do. Be tearing that shit up." Jazmine laughed.

"Exactly. Don't be a hater."

"Anyway," she dragged out. I'ma let you get back to being domestic. Hopefully, I won't see you soon."

"What? Why wouldn't you see me?" Amira asked, carefully unwrapping the chicken pastilla, a Moroccan delicacy, she removed from the oven.

Her mouth watered at the sweet, savory smell.

"Because... you're not homeless, and you have shelter now," Jazmine said. Amira was initially confused until she squinted, recalling their conversation at Juvie's.

She laughed and hissed after trying to remove a piece of the crust. "I'm not hiding under his balls." She snorted.

"You need to do something, hell. Make up for lost time and live in that man's skin."

Jazmine's suggestion didn't sound bad. The making up for lost time part. Living in his skin required her to touch him in ways Amira wasn't sure she was ready for.

"Just for you, I'll try cuddling with him tonight," Amira said.

"With your clothes off. Ass to pelvis, ma'am. You just had your laser appointment a few days ago, too. Put that pussy to use before it goes to waste."

Amira screamed. "Get the hell off my phone!"

Laughing, Jazmine said, "Don't say I never gave you any good advice. Bye."

"Bye, girl."

Amira tapped the screen, ending the call, and chuckled to herself. One thing Jazmine was going to do since they became friends was have Amira weak with laughter. She navigated the heavy topics with her, too, because life wasn't a joke, and she didn't play about people's mental health—especially those she loved. Amira would chalk it up to the social worker in her, but she knew that was Jazmine's heart regardless of her profession. The girl was a true gem and friend.

"Mm, mm. This is about to be so good," Amira mumbled.

She slid the knife into the flaky crust dusted with powdered sugar and cinnamon. While she should've waited for it to cool down, she was too hungry to wait. Perfectly seasoned chicken, sweet almonds, and spiced herbs were all she smelled as she plated a large slice.

Cutting a small piece, she popped it into her mouth and quickly blew out steam to cool her mouth down. Her eyes fluttered shut as the favors melted in her mouth. Sweet, savory, buttery—it was *everything.*

"I can't believe he made this for me," she mumbled, eating another piece.

Saleem knew anything pastry-like was her comfort food. He'd gone out of his way to prepare it before he went to the gym, and Amira was grateful. It was the small things that meant the biggest.

"He's going to spoil me, for real," she mumbled but loud enough.

"Nothing wrong with that."

Her head whipped around, eyes wide and glued on Saleem, who stood on the opposite side of the island. His gym bag was slung over his shoulder, and a skully was on his head. She noticed the extra shine on his skin from his workout as his fitted tee clung to his body.

"Saleem!" she said, clutching her chest. Her surprise melted quickly into a playful glare. "You can't be sneaking up on me like that!"

Chuckling, his gaze locked on her like she was the only thing in the world worth laying eyes on. "How am I sneaking up when I live here, too?"

Amira huffed but couldn't hide the smile tugging at her lips. "You know what I mean. I thought you were still at the gym. I didn't even hear you come in."

The garage was on the other end of the house.

"I was," he said, sliding his bag off his shoulder and approaching her. "Can't stay there all night, Angel."

Amira playfully rolled her eyes, watching his movements like a hawk. Saleem had been compliant, keeping his hands to himself for the most part. His lips were another story. Any chance he got, he was kissing Amira's neck, cheek, shoulder, and those soft lips he couldn't get enough of.

Amira held her breath when he came to stand

beside her, trying to deprive herself of his smell. Something about the way his workout musk blended with his natural scent awakened every filthy thought in her brain. Plus, she was ovulating, so her senses were heightened, and her body was on fire. Amira was ready to chain her wrists and ankles and put a muzzle over her mouth so she wouldn't growl when he kissed that spot on her neck right below her ear.

"What's up, baby?" Saleem said coolly. "It's good?"

He knew the answer, but he loved hearing and seeing her reactions. Her eyes fluttered as his scent and body heat blanketed her. Her heart did an aerial twist whenever he got too close or stared too long.

"Hey. Yes, it's delicious."

To keep busy, Amira forked another portion. Saleem watched her take a bite, a hum of appreciation slipping out, and he licked his lips. He could watch her eat all day.

"You knew that already, though," Amira said, putting a bit of space between them so she could look at his face. The pointed look she gave him made Saleem smirk.

"Just wanted to hear you say it."

"Fishing for compliments?"

Smirking, he shook his head. "Nah. Not fishing...just enjoying the view."

That made her pause her chewing, but pick her fork up and dig for another piece. "Right. Want a taste?"

Amira realized her poor choice of words the second they left her mouth, and Saleem nodded.

"Mm-hmm," he murmured, stepping her way, eliminating the space she created.

Amira held her fork out to him, but Saleem didn't move to take the bite. Instead, he slid closer, so close she could feel the heat radiating from him. "Nah," he said, his voice dropping even lower. "I didn't mean the food."

Before she could register his words, as if her mushed brain would let her, Saleem lowered his head to kiss lips that Amira had unconsciously puckered to receive him. His hand, gently but possessively, gripped the back of her neck, damn near able to close his hand. Her breath got caught in her throat, and she moaned when his tongue slid into her mouth.

The fork slipped from her hand, clattering softly against the counter as her hands instinctively found their way to his chest. His kiss wasn't rushed—it was deliberate like he was savoring her, taking his time to remind her of everything she tried not to feel about him.

Amira's knees weakened as his free hand rested on her waist, pulling her closer until there was no space between them. He tasted the faint taste of cinnamon and sugar in her mouth as he rolled his tongue around it, but nothing compared to the sweet whimpers she let out.

When he finally pulled back, Saleem rested his forehead against hers. Their breaths mingling and chests heaving. Amira's eyes fluttered open, and her cheeks flushed.

"Saleem..." she whispered, her voice barely audible.

He smiled, his thumb grazing her bottom lip. "What?"

She shook her head, trying to gather herself. "I thought you wanted the pastilla."

"I did," he said softly, his eyes dark with affection. "That was you giving me a taste."

Amira sighed. She was so turned on she couldn't think or see straight.

"You're... breaking my rules."

"Ain't no rules. You're mine," he said with that same smooth confidence, leaning in to steal one more kiss, this one softer.

Amira's only rebuttal was a shake of her head, which wasn't convincing at all. "Sure."

"I'ma go hop in the shower," he said.

"I'm coming with you."

His eyes widened at the outburst she thought she said in her head. Shielding her embarrassment with a hand covering her face, Amira shook her head.

"Aye." Saleem chuckled, stunned and humored by her response.

"Byyye. I meant I was going to stay down here and wait for you."

She was a flustered, horny mess. If he reached his hand in her pants right now, his hand would've come out dripping. Saleem didn't want to keep teasing her, knowing she wasn't *really* trying to take it there. He was seconds away from fucking her atop their brand-new counter, the island, or the table. It didn't matter where at, but he gave her a break.

"You sure you don't want to keep me company? You can wait in our bedroom," he said, grinning.

Amira eyed his firm pecs and the print in his sweats, and she almost slobbered down her chin. "No."

His eyebrow quirked, and she smirked, knowing what he was waiting for.

"Non, merci, Saleem," she said, telling him no thank you.

He smirked. "Yeah... that's what you better have said. You got lucky. If you need me, you know where to find me. I won't take too long."

She swallowed hard and, once he was out of earshot, whispered, "*Please* do. Fuck."

She fanned her face with both hands before running them through her hair and chuckling. She no longer cared about the rules or that damn pastilla, even though it was *so* good. Clearly, they'd continue to get broken, and nothing tasted better than his tongue in her mouth.

"You good?" Saleem's voice broke the silence in their bedroom.

Amira figured one night of sleeping in here with him wouldn't hurt, but she was sadly mistaken. She had stayed downstairs for as long as she could before Saleem came to retrieve her himself. After he scarfed down damn near half of the pastilla, listening to her tell him about her day, they retreated upstairs.

She wanted to sleep on the couch and put some distance between them for the night, but Saleem wasn't having it. Nor was he going to mess his back up by sleeping there. He promised to keep his hands to himself, and Amira wished he was a liar. When he stepped out of the bathroom with a white fluffy towel around his waist, body wet, hair fuzzy from the humidity, and stood in the doorway looking like sex itself... Amira melted into the sheets.

She'd showered in the guest bathroom to avoid him, yet that was a fail. Saleem had been courteous enough to slip on his sleep pants out of view, but that didn't matter. Amira had already gotten a glimpse of what he was working with. Not like she hadn't experienced the dick before, but that was young man pipe back then. Everything about Saleem was in a different league now.

So, Amira lay beside him, struggling to keep her urges to straddle his lap or his face down. She rolled onto her side for the fifth time, letting out exaggerated huffs with each twist. No matter how she turned, her body protested. There was nothing wrong with the mattress. It felt like she was sleeping on clouds the way it molded to her body, but her muscles were sore.

The day and week had taken more out of her than she realized, and sharing a bed with Saleem only added to her restless energy.

"Mhm," she mumbled, answering his question while staring at his side profile.

Saleem lay on his back with one arm casually dropped over his chest with his eyes closed. The durag on his head only added to his sexy sleep attire, which was just pants and no shirt. Amira was thankful for the minuscule glimmer of light given to ogle him.

"You sure? Is the bed uncomfortable? We can go test out a new one tomorrow," Saleem suggested.

Her bottom lip poked out, and she squeezed her thighs together. She was beside him, tossing and turning because she wanted him to put her through this bitch, and he was concerned about her comfort. *Yeah, I should give him some pussy.* The thought immediately came to her mind, and she snickered.

"Angel," he said, rolling over to face her.

She quickly shut her eyes. "The bed is alright," she lied, while her body screamed otherwise.

Saleem smirked but stayed quiet. When she

dramatically stretched and touched his hairy leg, she quickly scooted back some.

"You've been fighting with the mattress for the past twenty minutes," he teased. She could hear the smirk in his voice. "What's wrong?"

"Nothing," she lied again, but her body betrayed her when she groaned again.

Saleem sat up, leaning over to turn on the lamp. Flipping the covers back, he climbed out of bed and padded to the bathroom. The light flicked on and then turned off before Amira could see what he was doing. Her eyes looked everywhere but his face before they landed on a sleek black bottle with a pump in his hand.

"What's that?" she asked as he came to her side of the bed.

"Massage oil. You're sore."

It wasn't a question, but she nodded anyway.

"Um, yeah," she hesitated. "A little bit. You know... all this moving and stuff."

"Turn over," he said, his tone soft but firm.

"What?"

"Turn...over. Let me help you out."

Amira pinned him with questioning eyes. She marveled at his golden-brown skin and muscular arms that made her stomach qualify for the

Olympics. Her clit was the newest member of a rock band that only played drums the way it thudded.

"Please," Saleem added gently.

Their two-second stare-off ended, and Amira sighed, relenting to his request. Saleem tugged the cover away from her frame, getting a view of her thick thighs in the cotton shorts she had on. Paired with them was a thin tank top covering bare breasts. Saleem caught a glimpse of her swollen nipples before she rolled over onto her stomach, sliding her arms underneath the pillow. She heard him blow out an audible breath as her cheeks jiggled, and she held back her laugh.

"Shit don't make no sense," he grumbled lowly, shaking his head.

"What'd you say?" she asked, teasing him.

If she knew how hard his dick was, she'd stop while she was ahead. Saleem didn't bother to answer her. Instead, he moved closer to the bed. He wanted to give her the full experience, and her clothes restricted that.

"Um," he said and cleared his throat.

"What's wrong?"

He scratched his beard. "You mind taking your shirt off? I won't be able to really massage you the way I want to with it on."

He heard her suck in a breath. *The way I want to.* Amira was sure Saleem had no idea how erotic his words sounded; how personal he made them feel.

"That makes sense," she said before sliding her arms through the holes of her tank top and tossing it to the side. She got back comfortable, turning her head to face him. "Better?"

Saleem's eyes were glued to her smooth skin, vibrant tattoos he wanted to trace with his tongue, her visible love handles, and the taunting dip in her back. This view was *much* better.

"Yeah. Thank you."

Smiling, Amira turned her head, but not before eyeing his erection. "You're welcome."

Her hearing was heightened, honing in on every move he made. The sound of the oil being pumped into his hand made her chest heave. Her toes tingled when Saleem rubbed his palms together, providing a calming smell of lavender, lemon, and vanilla. The oil warmed immediately in his hands, and when they grazed her neck, she almost came.

Slowly, Saleem worked his fingers down her spine before concentrating on her shoulders. His fingers kneaded her muscles, ensuring he didn't miss any tension. Her skin was so soft, that Saleem massaged one area longer than intended. He worked out the knots in her shoulder with an expertise Amira didn't expect. The soft sigh that escaped her lips showed her gratitude.

"Mm," she let out.

"Let me know if it's too much," he said lowly, his breath brushing against her ear.

She shuddered.

"Um, can you turn on some music?" she asked out of the blue.

Saleem was puzzled for a split second by her request but did as she asked. Amira knew she couldn't lay through this massage if she had to listen to his heavy, controlled breaths.

"Yeah. Alexa...play Late Night playlist on shuffle," Saleem called out.

The virtual assistant knew exactly what time it was with the song of choice. *Love You Down* by Silk floated through the speaker at a low volume, further setting the mood. Saleem got back to the task at hand.

"That's good?" he asked, referring to the music.

Amira's bonnet-covered head moved across the satin pillowcase as she nodded. His hands reacquainted themselves, traveling down her back. Needing a bit more control, Saleem lifted her almost limp body into the middle of the bed. Then, she felt the bed dip, and his legs splayed on either side of her. Her breath hitched.

"This okay?" he asked, voice quiet and intimate.

"Yes," Amira damn near moaned.

Asking for consent was so damn attractive, and she was ready to give him complete dominance over her body. Warm palms worked the curve of her back, and she arched into his touch. The combination of pressure and tender care was almost hypnotic. The music had her ready to roll her hips. Saleem tended to her lower back, pressing his thumbs in the faint of her dimples. When a thumb grazed the crack of her ass, Amira lifted her hips more.

"You want to take these off, too?" Saleem asked, his breaths weighty.

His hands lingered on the band of her shorts. Amira's nod was short but received. Scooting down the bed, Saleem pulled the shorts over her ass in a slow drag. He clenched his jaw, running his tongue over his bottom lip. Grabbing the oil, he pumped more into his hand.

Firmly, he pressed into the backs of her thighs, moving his hands up to the cuff of her ass. The motion caused her cheeks to spread, giving him a teasing glimpse of her sticky center. Amira was so aroused that Saleem saw her clear essence stretch.

Keeping his composure, Saleem pressed kisses up her spine.

"You relaxed?" His voice was raspy, in concentration.

Saleem knew if he just focused on the experience and not how hard his dick was or how sweet her pussy smelled, he wouldn't end up giving her a happy ending.

"Mmhmm," she murmured, voice thick with need. "Keep going."

His fingers dug into her back and paused when Amira gave him clearer, different instructions.

"Touch me, *please*."

She didn't have to beg... not yet. Following orders, Saleem squeezed and massaged her ass, making it jiggle. His fingers glided over her slickness as a song by a talented baldheaded R&B singer crooned about making a girl tell him what she wanted from him. Saleem wasn't sure what Amira wanted before, but he was positive now.

He kissed her cheeks, the inside of her thighs, and then her lips before lifting her hips so that she was on her knees, spread open for him. The glossiness instantly covered his mouth. Amira sucked in a sharp breath as he slurped on her lips, cleaning the mess she made, only for him to create an even bigger one.

He smacked her ass, and then she felt her cheeks spread and warm saliva coat her asshole. Then, it was his tongue. Thick and hot, it probed her ass, dipping in before Saleem moved downward. He lapped at her clit with firm flicks and then sucked on it until Amira's body resembled the pouch of a Capri Sun once the juice was gone.

"Oh, my goooosh."

Amira's hands clenched the sheets as he wrote his name on her pussy... in Arabic. Then, French, then, in the only language she spoke fluently. Somehow, that made her shout it.

"Saleem!"

Thick fingers slid inside her while his lips stayed glued. Saleem massaged her gushy walls as he continued to eat her through a soul-extracting orgasm.

"Turn over," Saleem said, giving her no time to come down.

He gently laid her on her back, being greeted by large titties and dark brown areolas and nipples that made him dip his head for a taste. He sucked on a nipple and pinched the other one to a pointy peak. Amira's body arched away from the bed when he lowered his head back between her legs. Saleem wrapped his arms around her thighs, forcing her body back into the mattress. His tongue circled her clit, and he hummed in utter fulfillment.

"Baby," Amira called out shakily, clawing at his hand.

His response? A powerful suction around her bud that snatched her breath from her body and then filled it with a long gasp. Gluttony was a sin, and Saleem vowed to repent later. Allah knew his heart. Right now, all he wanted to do was overeat and overcompensate with nothing but firm licks and hard slurps to her center. He was apologizing to her pussy for letting so much time come in between them.

When she came again, Saleem finally lifted for air with wet lips and a soaked chin and beard that he could've wiped away with the back of his hand and flung. But he didn't do that. That'd be much too selfish of him, and he was a selfless man. A pleasing lover. A giver and provider. It'd be a shame if he went against his morals. Leaning over her quaking frame, Saleem kissed her open mouth as she struggled to catch her breath.

"You taste so fucking good, Angel," he rasped, kissing her again.

Amira sucked on his tongue and reached between them. He put up no protest when she shoved his pants down, gripped his heavy dick, and placed it at her opening. She didn't even stroke him. She didn't need to. Amira wanted him inside her. Saleem trembled when he slid in.

"Sa...uuuh." She couldn't get his name out.

Not when he stroked her fully and pulled out. Then, he repeated the motion while lifting her legs. It was feeling too good, too fast. Amira's eyes fluttered.

"A condom," she said, finally remembering common sense.

Nothing about them was typical, though. He had no sense when it came to her... when it came to them. Saleem's nostrils flared as she tightened around him.

"I'd never play with your life like that. I'm clean."

She nodded, and he pressed her thighs back into the bed. Amira trusted him wholeheartedly. He kept eye contact as he glided in and out of her. His strokes were long and purposeful, almost punishing as their skin clapped loudly. Jazmine would be happy to know that she put ass to pelvis...just in a different position.

"Your pussy *so* fucking tight," Saleem grunted, upset and pleased all at once.

His eyes crossed when she started fucking him back, rotating her hips to meet thrust that had Saleem placing a hand at her neck. Amira smiled when he squeezed.

"You ain't have no fucking business keeping this pussy from me," he hissed, pounding into her.

The smile was wiped smooth off her face. "I'm sorry!"

"Louder."

"I'm *so* sorry, baby!" Her exclamation put a soprano to shame.

Saleem applied more pressure, spreading her legs wider and going deeper. Nothing but savage thrusts to remind her who the fuck he was and how he gave it up. His face lowered, a hot breath floating across her damp skin. Throaty words spoken in French made her squirt, and then he repeated them.

"This is *my* pussy, Angel. Tell me."

Amira screamed. "It's yours! Oh, my fucking... it's yooours!

Saleem was close. Her moans and whimpers made him surrender restraint. It'd been a minute, but he wanted to give her his best. Her wet lashes, flushed cheeks, and dripping pussy said he'd done a stupendous job. Some of his best fucking work to date. Saleem deserved a medal around his neck; Amira around his neck. A master key to her soul; fuck the city. The city didn't know him like she did.

Years apart meant nothing now. This wasn't just them reconnecting. This was soul-tying, mind-fusing, heart-pounding lovemaking.

His face crinkled, and his hands squeezed her hips. "Ssss... *fuck*."

A hiss slipped through clenched teeth as his nut appeared. Amira contracted around him, making sure he emptied every drop. Saleem came hard and long, coating her walls like he wanted her to feel him for the rest of her life. And... that was the plan.

What were those rules that she mentioned?

"YOU WERE GOING TO BE MY WIFE REGARDLESS."

EIGHT

"I'm sorry." Quinn chuckled. "You said you agreed to do what?" she asked, staring at the screen of her phone.

Sighing, Amira repeated herself, "To marry Saleem."

"Yeah... I think I heard that part. What I didn't hear was why?"

After Quinn started questioning her about the way she'd been acting, Amira figured she might as well tell her the truth. She had already let Jazmine in on the ordeal.

"It's a favor," she answered with a shrug, like marrying him meant nothing.

As if Saleem had only been tossing dick in her guts and down her throat for damn near a month straight to show his appreciation. Amira felt like she could taste his cum every time she burped. They'd been having the grandest time in the sheets, but it was time to get serious. Sex could wait.

Quinn shook her head. "That's some favor after all these years."

"Yeah, I know," she said, somewhat regretting that she told her.

Amira didn't know why she wanted her to be happy. She didn't know why it even mattered because this wasn't a real marriage.

"You're glowing, though—my goodness," Quinn said, blinking rapidly.

Then her phone lowered, and Amira was stuck staring at the ceiling.

"Quinn," Amira called out. "Are you... are you crying?"

"No." She sniffled. "I got something in my eye."

Amira smirked and studied her face when she came back into view. "Awww. Are those tears happy ones?"

"Of course, they are. You aren't seeing what I see, Mira. Even hearing the way you've been talking these last few weeks. It all makes sense now."

"What does?"

"You're in love."

Amira sputtered a laugh. "No, I'm not."

She wasn't convincing at all.

"So, what do you call it then?" Quinn was curious to know.

"I told you...a favor. You know I had to be out of my place, and he offered me his home in exchange for taking his last name," Amira explained.

Quinn rubbed her eye, wanting to say more, but she didn't. "I don't really think that required you to move in, but I'm happy regardless of what you think this is."

Amira laughed. "You're the one trying to make it more than what it is."

"Says the sparkle in your eye and hickey on your neck."

Her hands flew around her neck, not knowing which side Quinn was talking about. Saleem had been so in the moment, so deep inside her, that sucking on every inch of her body was automatic. Her titties were decorated along with the insides of her thighs, where he'd gotten a little rough before bathing her. Amira's clit thumped at the flashback.

"You're lying," Amira whispered.

"And so are you." Quinn smiled. "So, when can I start planning?"

Amira ignored her question while she dug

around in her purse for her compact mirror. She was too old to be walking around like she lived with a blood-sucking vampire. Well, technically, he was a sucker. One that collected souls. Amira had never had her pussy eaten so good in her life.

Turning her head from side to side, seeing clear skin, Amira snapped the mirror shut. "You know... I don't really want a big wedding. I don't even think we have time for all of that."

"Huh? What do you mean?" Quinn asked.

"So... we have to tie the knot when his dad returns home in a month. I think we have about a month left," she mumbled, opening the calendar on her desktop.

That shocked Quinn, and she couldn't hide it if she tried. "Now, see. That has me wanting to retract what I said."

"About?"

"About this being more. Did he make you sign a contract or something?"

She shook her head. "No. He said there was no need for one. If I wanted one to be drawn up, I could."

"But you don't," Quinn guessed.

"Nope. By the time a year is up, I'll have my own

home, and we can continue to fake it. It's not like I asked to walk away with something."

Quinn sucked her teeth, concern flashing in her wide eyes. "You should've. So, all you get out of this is a place to lay your head and some dick?"

"No." Amira huffed, rolling her eyes. "Am I not grown? You sound like—"

"Please don't say that mother of yours because eww. Hell no," Quinn spat.

She didn't care that Evelyn was her aunt or her mama's sister. She couldn't stand that lady and would beat her ass off GP.

"I wasn't going to say that. I was going to say you sound like I made a bad decision," Amira explained.

"I don't mean for it to sound that way, but you know I have to ask questions. I'm glad that Saleem saw a need and wasted no time stepping up, and even happier that you accepted."

After a bunch of pushback, Amira thought.

"But?" Amira pressed. She knew there was more. There always was with Quinn.

"But...I want you to keep it real with yourself. This is Saleem we're talking about. He was your first true love, and the nigga pops up out of nowhere asking for you to be his wife? I don't know. It's a little fishy. Does he owe folks some money or something? Niggas ain't gon' try to kidnap you, are they?"

Amira chuckled. "Please stop watching Tubi and Lifetime."

"Girl, please. They be having some good shit on there. You and Saleem need to pitch this situation to them for a script. Bet it'd do numbers."

"I'm not about to play with you."

Quinn shrugged. "Can't say I never tried to put you on."

They chuckled, and Amira tried to ease her cousin's worries.

"Trust me, I know what I've gotten myself into, okay? I'm being taken care of on every level, and that's how it'll go until the year is up. Nothing more, nothing less."

With pursed lips, Quinn said, "Okay. And if this turns into something more before then, you owe me a hundred dollars."

Amira waved her off. "That's chump change."

"Yeah... we'll see, Ms. Big Money." Quinn chuckled, knowing in her heart that she was about to be one hundred dollars richer real soon.

Amira entered Jennie Mae's, and a smile immediately covered her face, reaching her eyes. Seeing Saleem's hard work by way of the customers scattered about and in line made her not as regretful for having ended things back then. In her mind, Amira knew their lives would've been entirely different had she not had the courage to go separate ways, but she tried not to harp on the past. Only the future, and that's why she was here. After talking with Quinn, Amira realized they didn't have as much time to plan as she thought. With the way life had stressed her out months ago, she wasn't in the mood for a repeat—favor or not.

"Aye, how you doing? Welcome in." Amira heard to her right.

She turned her head, eyes landing on a young man with long locs rocking an olive-green Jennie Mae's work shirt.

"Hey. I'm good. Thank you." She smiled.

Amira took in the space, loving how beautifully

inviting it was. The pictures of Jennie Mae and her recipes on the wall made her wonder about the legacy she would leave behind. She wasn't sure what song was playing over the speakers, but the bobbing of people's heads let her know it was a hit. She liked the beat, too. Pulling out her phone, Amira swiped down on the right of the screen and tapped the Shazam circle to get the song's name. Her head jerked back when the title *In Fate We Trust* by Laurent popped up.

"What the..." she mumbled, saving the song to her music library with plans to spin it back when she got in the car.

Locking her phone, she moved up in line with a smirk on her face. A few customers occupied tables, sipping from bottles or cups filled with juices or a smoothie. She wasn't sure what she'd be ordering, and she should've taken the time to read over the menu, but her focus was on the man behind the counter.

Saleem stood near the back with black gloves on, slicing a pineapple. His forearms flexed with each cut, and Amira found him being in his element so attractive. When he glanced up after placing the chunks in a clear-lidded container, his eyes locked on her, and a slow smile crept across his face. Heat pooled in the pit of Amira's stomach, tightening her nipples.

He looked so good in his unbuttoned khaki shirt with a large Jennie Mae logo on the back, wrapped turban, and dark denim jeans. Amira caught the Polo logo on the hem of his white shirt, covering what she knew was a wife-beater underneath. She mentally counted how long it'd take to get him out of all three so she could rub her hands across his body.

Saleem held up a finger her way, mouthing for her to *hold on, baby*. He washed his hands after removing his gloves and stalked her way. There her stomach went tumbling again. He spoke to a few customers and approached her in the steadily moving line.

"Hey," she said, engulfed in his embrace before she could fully get the word out.

Amira reciprocated, and when he went to kiss her lips, she pulled back some. Saleem screwed his face up.

"What was that?" he asked.

"Huh?"

His head dipped, bringing lips close to her ear. "You don't want me kissing you now?"

Saleem gave her an inch of space to see her face. Amira blinked, and a nervous grin appeared.

"In front of all these people?" she asked in a whisper, stretching her eyes as if to relay a message that they shared, but Saleem hadn't received it.

Then, he got it. But he didn't convey he understood that she was tossing around her, *this doesn't mean we're together...like romantically*, bullshit she stated weeks ago. Saleem just nodded, and she could immediately feel the distance between them. It was all in the way he addressed her next.

"You want a smoothie or a juice?"

His voice held no malice. It was a valid question. An even playing field inquiry that sided heavily with Amira's nothing more, nothing less rhetoric. She didn't like that too much now.

"Um," she hesitated, not giving a damn about either one. "No. I'm okay. I actually came up here to talk to you about something."

"A'ight, let's go to my office real quick," Saleem suggested.

Before they could step away, Lune swaggered their way with a grin on his handsome baby face.

"You ain't getting nothing?" he asked Amira.

She shook her head. "Maybe when I leave out. What's the best juice?"

Lune glanced back at the colorful chalkboard menu that he had yet to learn. "Shit...that Bunny drink is kinda coo'."

Amira's eyes found Saleem's, wanting him to explain the meaning behind the name.

"It's a carrot, apple, and grapefruit juice," he shared.

"Ooh. That sounds good," Amira said.

Lune nodded. "Yeah. I fuck with it."

Saleem gave him a deadpan stare, grilling him about his language. No words were necessary.

"My fault. Come find me when you're about to leave. I'll hook you up," Lune offered.

Amira smirked, watching a storm pass through Saleem's eyes. Lune gave Saleem a big smile before heading behind the counter. Saleem shook his head, not the least bit humored by Lune trying to charm Amira when she just played in his face.

"Come on," Saleem said, a hand at the small of her back, guiding her toward the hallway.

He opened the door to his office, and Amira stepped inside. It smelled like him, and Amira inhaled. A wall of open blind windows bathed the room with natural lighting, allowing her to tour the space easily.

His desk sat in the center. A matte black piece

with a glass top reflected light just right. Polished concrete offset the sleek, modern feel yet gave it an edge that Amira loved. A sense of calmness washed over her after spotting the indoor water fountain. The sound was so serene. A massive picture of Saleem, his family, friends, and his team of people who helped make Jennie Mae's more than a business hung from the wall behind his desk. It was a snapshot of him cutting the ribbon at the grand opening.

"It's so cozy in here," Amira commented, sitting in one of the plush gray chairs. "I wasn't expecting this."

Saleem walked around to sit facing her at the edge of his desk. "Expected beanbags and a basketball hoop?"

Her lips quirked into a smile. "No... but it fits you. Very polished and sophisticated. I'd stay in here all day."

Saleem snuffled, amused by her sharp observation skills, yet she failed to pick up on the change between them.

He crossed his arms at the wrists, locking eyes on her pretty face. "So, do I pass your inspection?"

"Barely," she teased. "Is this where you spend most of the day?"

"For the most part, unless I'm on the go or out of town."

Amira nodded, loving how much of a boss he was. There wasn't an arrogant bone in his body.

"That's nice. You have me wanting to redecorate mine now," she said in a whine that wasn't meant to make Saleem's chest tight.

Digging into his pocket, he removed a small knot of money, and his hand extended her way. Amira looked at it and then at him.

"Redecorate," he said, pushing the bills to his fingertips for her to accept.

"Like that?"

He smirked. "Ain't it always been that way?"

Amira grabbed the knot, stuffing it in her purse. "Thank you."

"You're welcome. What's up, though? You said you needed to talk to me about something," he said.

That quickly, she'd gotten off track. Her mind created scenarios as to why he was walking around with *that* kind of money on a Tuesday. Then, she thought back to what Quinn had insinuated, and her posture shifted, then her eyes squinted with wonderment.

"What?" Saleem asked.

"This money," she said, head titling to her purse. "Is it legal?"

"Legally mine, yes."

Her mouth opened and closed slowly. Saleem didn't elaborate until he saw her swallow as if she was doing her best to keep from throwing up.

"Someone owed me."

"Oh!" she exclaimed. "Okay. And *you* don't owe anyone, right?"

Saleem chuckled. "Angel, what are you getting at?"

"Do you?" she asked, her voice sterner.

"No. I've never owed anyone a day in my life."

Saleem watched her shoulders drop, and he gritted his teeth. Someone had gotten into her head about him, and he didn't like that.

"Okay... good to know." She sighed. "Now, what I came to talk about was the wedding."

His mood shifted instantly. "Yeah? What about it?"

"So, remember how you told me it's usually tradition to have a three-day ceremony for weddings?" He nodded, the corners of his mouth almost lifting into a smile as he recalled her excitement and curiosity during their late-night conversation. "I don't really want to do that."

His brows lifted slightly, but he didn't seem surprised. "No family? No friends?"

"Saleem," she said softly, finally looking at him. "This whole thing...it's not exactly traditional."

He studied her for a moment, trying to figure something out, but couldn't quite place what just yet.

"Okay. We can do whatever you want," he said easily.

"Are you sure? We can always do it big later."

Now, she studied him, waiting to see if he felt she was coming off as disrespectful for her suggestion. Saleem hadn't been surer about anything in a while. About anyone. This *thing* between them was undeniable—raw and unfiltered, hitting him harder than he thought possible. So, if she wanted to skip out on all the grand festivities for now, that's what she'd get.

"Baby, we can go to the courthouse or exchange vows at the crib today. As long as you're not overwhelmed more than I'm sure I already have you, it's whatever. *You* tell me if you're sure about this."

Her head bobbed passively. "Yes."

The word had never sounded sweeter. Saleem smirked. "Say it again."

Amira playfully rolled her eyes and chuckled. "Here we go. Don't start anything in this office, Mr. Majid."

Saleem licked his lips, loving how his last name rolled off her tongue. Soon, he'd get to address her with the same name... as his wife. That thought alone made him lengthen in his pants. Amira's eyes shifted to him adjusting himself, and she smirked. *I'll have to call him that more often,* she thought.

"I'll try my best not to. I know you need a break." His voice dipped lower, reaching in between her legs.

He was tempting her, wanting to see just how far he could take it. Just how nasty she'd let him be. Fucking her in his office wasn't the wildest thing. It didn't come close to the different ways he wanted to turn her out. Saleem could give her a list to check off.

Amira ran a hand over her head, down to the tips of her curly ends. "The wedding can be small. Something intimate. Just us and a few witnesses." She needed them to regroup before things got real.

"Yeah... I'm coo' with that 'cause I didn't want to share you with a crowd anyway. Not yet. We can make our own traditions. Start fresh. No rules, no expectations. Just us."

She nodded, fully in agreeance. "No outside influences to sway our decision."

"*Your* decision," he clarified. "You were going to

be my wife regardless. The stipulations just added a bit of excitement, but know you were always going to have my last name. In this life and the next."

Amira wanted to respond; she really did. Saleem always seemed to leave her momentarily speechless, with her brain void of coherent thoughts. The weight of his words and the conviction in his smooth voice, made every doubt about them disappear.

"And all this was going to happen without even knowing where I was or who I was with?" Amira had to tease him.

He looked down at her hand. "Considering how bare that finger is, you weren't with a nigga that was 'bout shit. Damn, sure wasn't worth shit since you're here with me. Don't worry, though... it's gon' be sitting heavy real soon."

She tucked her lips, smiling. Glancing down at her hand, she couldn't believe this was about to happen. It all felt surreal. This man, his love, and the way he looked at her like she was the only thing worth living for. Amira could try to convince herself that this wasn't real all she wanted to; Saleem was going to make her face the truth.

"Will your parents be upset? Your dad specifically?" Amira asked.

Saleem shook his head. "Nah. I mean, my mama

and sisters might be pissed. My dad is chill. He just wants to see me happy."

"Oh. I make you happy?" Amira asked cautiously.

Saleem hadn't stopped grinning and showing his pretty ass teeth since she came back into his life.

"Very. I'd be even happier if you gave me a kiss," he said, smirking.

Chuckling, Amira stood up. She stepped in between his legs, and Saleem held her face in both hands. She grinned so hard her eyes closed some.

"You're so damn pretty, and you're all mine," he said, kissing her lips. "You ready to be my wife?"

She smiled against his lips, running the tip of her tongue up them. "Oui," she answered, telling him yes in French.

Amira leaned more into his body, ready to slide her tongue into his mouth, when Saleem delivered a hard smack to her ass that made her pussy cream.

"Baaaby," she whined.

Saleem stood up from the desk and turned her away from him. "Go lock the door, and then come get on your knees. If you get nasty with it like I like, I might bend your ass over this desk. As my wife, you don't get to dodge my kisses because people are around. Fuck them people."

Amira damn near sprinted to the door. He could've told her to crawl back to him, and she would've. Since she wanted to deny him of his second favorite set of lips, Saleem was about to put her mouth to work. All that wedding talk had him riled up, and whatever came next for them... whether she wanted to believe it or not, would be their *thing*. And that's all that mattered.

She was all that mattered to him.

9

"I THOUGHT I LOST YOU FOR GOOD."

NINE

Standing inside her closet in front of the full-length mirror, Amira ran her hands over the fabric of her dress for the third time in two minutes. Twisting her frame from side to side, she sighed. She was leaning toward changing but didn't really want to.

The soft, chocolate-brown material hugged her frame just right, highlighting her curves without doing too much. Gold hoops, a gold cross necklace, and her new gold watch, which Saleem bought her, set the outfit off. Chocolate and gold paired so well, but she was still second-guessing her outfit.

"Baby, do you think this is too much?" she called out for Saleem, frowning at her reflection.

He shook his head from their bedroom, though she couldn't see him. "I don't know, baby. Come here and let me see for the fifth time," he teased.

"Asshole," she grumbled and walked out of her closet into the bedroom.

Saleem was halfway through buttoning his shirt, standing there like the definition of tall, fine, and taken. His charcoal slacks sat perfectly on his hips, and his crisp white shirt had the top two buttons undone, exposing a chain that matched Amira's. He glanced up, hands pausing on his belt buckle as his eyes swept over her from head to toe. Slow and deliberate.

"Nah. You're good," he said casually, his lips twitching like he was fighting a grin.

"I'm good?" Amira rolled her eyes, putting her hands on her hips. "Don't play with me right now."

He smirked, adjusted the collar of his shirt, and walked over to her. "Do a spin for me," he said, grabbing her hand to twirl her around.

Amira did a 360, giving him a full view with a smile. When she was back facing him, he licked his lips.

"You look perfect," he said, his tone dropping into that smooth, velvety space that always made her stomach flip. "Like, I might have to tell folks that we can't make dinner 'cause I don't wanna share you tonight."

Amira's lips parted, and she blinked up at him, her faux irritation fading. "Saleem..."

"What?" He leaned in closer, his hands settling on her waist. "I mean it. You look good. *Real* good, baby." He jiggled her booty in his hands and kissed her neck.

That was the only place above her chest he was granted to kiss. Amira had done her makeup flawlessly, and she'd be damned if he messed it up.

She squirmed and let out a small laugh, swatting at his chest. "Stop trying to feel me up before we really don't make it. What if your mom thinks I'm doing too much?"

"She won't," he said firmly, his thumbs rubbing small circles against her sides. "But even if she did, I wouldn't care. You're with me...not anybody else. And besides," he added, his eyes dropping to her dress again, wanting to plant his face in her barely visible cleavage, "you ain't doing enough if you ask me. I was hoping for something to make my pops jealous."

Amira shook her head, laughing as she pushed

him back. "You play too much. Let me put on some perfume, and we can go."

He stepped back but gave her one last once-over, his grin widening. "Nah, for real, though. You look beautiful, Angel. Especially with your new jewels. Stop worrying."

She glanced down and smiled. "Okay, okay." She huffed, fluffing her curls. "Let's just hope everything goes good."

"It will. And if it gets too crazy, I'll say we gotta go 'cause I got the bubble guts or something."

Amira laughed again, shaking her head as she stepped inside her closet. "You're ridiculous."

"Yeah, but you love me," he shot back, waiting for her to deny his claim.

Amira smirked. "Mhm. I'm glad you know."

Once they were finally dressed, they headed to the garage. Saleem had a plethora of vehicles to choose from. One for almost every day of the week, but he loved his Cadillac, so that's what they hopped in. He held Amira's door open, making sure she was good before he closed it.

"You got everything?" he asked as she got comfortable.

"Yes."

He shut the door and walked around to his side.

Sliding into the driver's seat, Saleem lifted the garage and started the engine. Backing out, he thought about turning on some music but didn't. Their rides together lately had consisted of them talking, getting to know one another more. Saleem didn't mind that; conversations with her had always been the best.

And he knew what to expect when they died down. Playing passenger princess, Amira didn't waste a second before pulling her phone out once Saleem stopped talking. She was thankful for the distraction, but she had one of her own. He clocked the little smile on her face as she scrolled, tapping on something before angling the screen so he couldn't see.

"What you looking at?" he asked, glancing at her as he pulled onto the main street that led to the highway.

"Nothing," she said, her voice all sweet and innocent, but he wasn't buying it.

"Uh-huh. I already know."

Amira didn't respond; she just smirked and turned the volume up. Saleem couldn't hide his smile or control the onset of weird motions in his chest when he heard the beat drop to a song that'd been on loop in his mind for the past two weeks.

Beyoncé's warm, soulful voice floated through

the car as she sang *So Amazing*. Amira knew from the moment she heard the song that it would be the one she walked down the aisle to. Back then, she didn't know who she'd be meeting at the end of it, but that was no longer a question or a concern. She'd been playing the video back-to-back ever since the videographer sent it over. She watched it before they went to bed, when she was bored at work, and whenever her eyes landed on the wedding ring adorning her hand.

That was the new jewels Saleem mentioned in their bedroom. When Amira told him she'd be okay with exchanging their vows at home, Saleem rolled with it at the moment. He could see the uncertainty in her eyes that day in his office, though. She was doing this to get it over with, but Saleem wasn't feeling that.

So, he flew them to Barbados and changed her last name. Not just them but Quinn, Jazmine, and his brother, Rahim. He owed him a favor, and being a witness of their union was the best repayment. An all-expenses-paid trip, thanks to his older cousins, to solidify their love was one he'd do over and over again. When Saleem told her what he had planned, because surprising her would've caused way too much stress, Amira didn't put up a fight. She was tired of getting in her own way.

Enough time had gone by with them apart, and she didn't want to waste another minute of it without him. For his convenience or not, she placed her fear aside and became his wife. When she sniffled, Saleem glanced her way, and he already knew what part of the video she was on—the exchange of their vows.

They stood at the altar, hand in hand. Her hands and bare feet were beautifully decorated with henna. Though they hadn't gone the traditional way as planned, Amira still wanted to honor his culture. Her ivory-draped bodice with a cat-eye neckline emphasized her collarbone and gorgeous tattoos. The side split flowed with the waves while pearl buttons rained down the spine. Seeing her look like the angel he claimed her to be, took Saleem's breath away, but his voice, his loving words like always, left Amira breathless.

Saleem's deep, steady voice filled the car as her screen showed him holding a small card. He didn't bother to look at it at once when his eyes landed on her.

"Amira... my angel," he started, voice beyond thick with emotion. "I thought I lost you for good, but I should've known better. That's what I get for thinking I knew what love was. I thought it was supposed to be easy... something you stumble into and hope to keep. Then, we met and you wiped every idea of it out of my head."

"It's work. It's intention. It's choosing each other even when things aren't perfect but also letting each other go so we can grow. Maybe I wasn't prepared for you back then. I wasn't the man you thought could care for your heart as if it were mine. But that's the thing, baby... it is. I knew it from the moment we met, and I cracked a joke about you walking down the aisle to me one day. You laughed and still gave me your number."

The small party chuckled, and Saleem cleared his throat before continuing.

"It was always supposed to be us. I don't want to just coexist in your world. I want to live it with you. Experience every emotion, every sad day, the wins, the losses, the tears I know you gon' cry because you're my little softie." He smirked. "The happiness, Angel. *Your* happiness. I promise to be everything right in your world. To laugh with you. To cry with you and wipe your tears. To fight for us no matter what. Knock a nigga on his—" He paused and shook his head with a grin. "Y'all know what

I'm getting at. You're mine to protect and provide for. To learn who you are as a grown woman and take care of you...take care of your heart. I didn't just pray on this good thing between us. I prayed over it and for it. For you... for *us*. And I'll never stop. I'll forever love you like you deserve to be loved every single day of my life as long as you don't tell me no."

Amira's light makeup was absolutely ruined by the end of his vows. To be loved, seen, and heard had her bawling. She'd blamed herself so many nights for being young and not fully ready to accept a man who wanted to give her the world and still did. Saleem didn't come back into her life to selfishly break her heart like she'd done his. He gave it to her over and over because he knew that's what she needed. Saleem was mending wounds he hadn't caused but was determined to heal. He knew it wouldn't be easy, but it wasn't impossible.

The video zoomed in on Amira as Quinn lightly dabbed her face with a cloth. She didn't even care about the makeup anymore, but she needed to see. Saleem's hands squeezed hers as she sniffled, and that was all the push she needed.

Before the video could keep playing, she paused it and blew out a long breath.

"Why would you ever make me cry like that?" she muttered softly, half-laughing.

Saleem glanced at her from the corner of his eye, giving her an apologetic grin. "I was just telling you what's been on my heart, baby. Ain't that's what we were there for?"

Amira nodded, loving how he didn't tuck his feelings for her at any moment. When she hit play again, the video shifted to her vows.

"Saleem..." she started, her voice trembling. Amira took a deep breath, her fingers gripping his like they were her lifeline.

"I wasn't sure what I would say once I got up here but know that I love you. I never stopped and always will. How do I put into words what you mean to me when you've completely changed my life for the better? You showed me patience when I didn't even know how to give it to myself. You see me, I mean really *see* me, in a way no one else ever has. You've been my best friend, my peace, and my favorite person to argue with when you won't let me tell you no," she said, laughing through her tears, earning a chuckle from her girls.

"But more than anything, you've been my home. My peace, my—"

Her voice cracked, and Saleem did what he only

knew to do. Stepping forward, he cupped her face in his hands like he was anchoring her to him. Silently, with just his touch, he gave her the strength to keep going. He moved back in place, but not too far away.

"You've been everything I thought I wasn't ready for. You prepared me back then, and I promise to never take you for granted again. And to never forget how good your love feels. I promise to love you, to respect you, and to grow with you. Saleem, you're it for me. My last first kiss, my last everything. I can't wait to spend the rest of my life with you and continue showing you just how much you mean to me."

Saleem stood there like he'd just been hit with every emotion at once. Like the waves had come crashing down on him, swallowing him whole. His usual calm, collected aura was nowhere to be found. His jaw tightened, and his Adam's apple bobbed as he tried to keep his composure. His eyes twitched and glistened with unshed tears that he didn't try to hide as he stared at her. He stared into Amira's soul that fused with his years before now. *This* was what he prayed for.

Saleem's grip on her hands tightened. He needed her to be his anchor because her words had wrecked him in the best way possible. The man who never let anyone see him sweat but her, was coming undone, standing before her girls with his chest rising and falling as if he couldn't catch his breath. A tear rolled down his cheek when Amira quietly whispered, *I love you so much* in French.

Jazmine and Quinn let out a soft *aww*, wiping their tears, and Saleem snuffled while Rahim patted his shoulder. He shook his head as if it'd help pull himself together. His eyes never left Amira's that were so full of love and gratitude.

"You tryna embarrass me out here," he teased, voice rough but warm.

Everyone chuckled, but Amira caught the way his thumb gently stroked the back of her hand. It was him silently thanking her for loving him enough to be vulnerable with her. It was all he ever wanted.

The video ended, and Amira rubbed her lips together. "I was so scared that day," she admitted quietly.

"Scared of what?" Saleem asked, glancing her way.

"Messing everything up. Thinking you'd get cold feet. Saying the wrong thing... not being enough for you."

His eyes jerked away from the road, his expression softening. "You serious? Baby...you could've gotten up there and read the alphabet, and I would've still married you. You were already enough for me long before we said 'I do.'"

Her heart swelled at the sincerity in his voice. "You mean that?"

He nodded, his lips curving into a small smile. "Yes. Always. And you know what else?"

"What?" she asked, ready to listen to any and everything he had to say.

"I ain't put no music on 'cause I knew this is what you was gon' do," he teased, lightening the mood.

Amira laughed, swatting his arm. "You swear you know me."

"I do," he said, grinning now. "And I know by the time we pull up, you gon' be in the best mood with no nervous energy in sight. So, keep playin' your videos. We look good together."

She rolled her eyes but couldn't stop smiling as she focused back on her phone. Saleem glanced at her again, and he intertwined their hands. That was love. The sight of her so happy, so in love with them, didn't tighten his chest. It made it feel lighter than ever. She was his forever, and Saleem wouldn't have it any other way.

Amira had been nervous about meeting his parents again, for no reason, but Saleem understood why. She was the woman who'd broken their son's heart, and now she was his wife. Having reservations was warranted. They loved her, though. They even had all those years back.

Amira couldn't get over how beautiful his entire family was. Not just physically, but their aura. She could feel that they'd all been raised on love, something she was still getting used to.

Tiffany was skeptical at first, but she was a woman. She knew how difficult juggling life could be and having a boyfriend so young while chasing your dreams was a lot. She didn't judge her for ending things. She just hoped that she now knew what she wanted. Amira was glad she didn't hold a grudge because she needed the peach cobbler Saleem requested she make specifically for her every few weeks.

Tayah couldn't make it due to a modeling gig out of town, but Yuhani and Rahim were present, along with some of their male and female cousins and their families. Youssef had been waiting to see Amira the most and let it be known all night. She snuck away from everyone to catch a breather, and he found her in the kitchen while coming to get another plate of food.

"You hiding out already?"

She turned to see Youssef washing his hands at the sink before drying them and grabbing a new plate. Much like Saleem's, his presence was commanding but carried a warmth that made her feel at ease. He was just as handsome, too, with a salt-and-pepper beard, deep coal-black waves, and wheat-colored skin. Their children were a perfect blend of them, but Amira could tell Yuhani favored her mother more. Her milk chocolate skin was gorgeous.

"Not hiding," Amira said. "Just... regrouping."

Youssef chuckled and popped his plate into the microwave. "Ain't nothing wrong with that. This family can be a lot, but they're harmless. Mostly."

Amira laughed softly, nodding. "No harm was done. I just didn't know how everyone would feel about us being together."

Youssef's expression softened. He leaned against the counter, studying her for a moment. "Let me tell you something about my son," he began, his voice steady. "Saleem's always been the kind of man who thinks ten steps ahead. He's real careful about the people he lets close. So, if he's brought you here as his wife, there's nothing you need to be worried about. No test you need to try and pass."

Amira felt her cheeks heat, but she kept her gaze on him. Even when the microwave beeped, he removed his plate and grinned.

"My first daughter-in-law," he said.

Amira smiled. "I heard you've been waiting on one," she teased as he chewed his food.

Youssef chuckled. "Yeah, but I know my son. He wasn't rushing into anything for the sake of my wants. It's our values, but I'd view him as less of a man had he gone out and married some woman, who doesn't deserve his love and legacy. It means everything to me."

She simpered at his words. "Well, I'm glad you welcomed me with open arms."

"It's not like we hadn't before," he joked, and Amira lightly gasped.

"Oh, so Saleem gets his sarcasm from you? Got it. Let me go get Ms. Tiffany on you."

Youssef laughed, loving how she wasn't afraid to be silly and speak her mind with him. From being around her tonight and from what Saleem had told him while he was away, Amira was a real one. She moved with authenticity and didn't try to impress anyone but cared about others' feelings. Amira seamlessly fit in tonight, asking about their culture, listening to their stories, cracking jokes, and vibing with everyone, even though her nervousness sometimes seeped through. That kind of self-assuredness was something every parent valued in their child's partner.

"My wife knows what she got herself into marrying me. Tell her to bring my drink up here while she's at," Youssef said, chuckling.

"It was a pleasure tonight. Truly, Mr. Majid," Amira said.

Youssef shook his head. "Call me Youssef. We're family. And just so you know, I'm here for whatever you need as well. Me and Tiff are a call away. You understand?"

Amira's throat tightened, and she quickly nodded, too afraid that if she spoke, nothing but tears would come out.

"Good. You and Saleem are going to be just fine, but you can call me if he gets out of line."

She nodded again and lowly said, "Thank you."

Youssef dumped his plate and grinned. "Mmm,

hmm. Now, come on back downstairs before they think I helped you escape."

Amira chuckled. "I will. Let me use the bathroom."

"When you leave out of here, take the first right and go all the way back. You can't miss it but if you do, just press the intercom button by the steps."

She blinked, trying to wrap her mind around how casually he said that. Having a built-in intercom system in their home wasn't normal. *That's that Arab money,* she jokingly sang in her head and walked out of the kitchen.

On her way to relieve her bladder, Amira had to admit that she felt lighter. The nerves that had been sitting heavily in her chest for weeks now were gone and replaced with confidence, knowing that she'd found a family. Saleem's family as his wife at that.

"Look at God," she mumbled.

Then, her brows dipped. She was so caught up in her newfound happiness that she missed a turn. Or was it two? Amira wasn't sure, so she turned around and decided to head back downstairs. Those were her intentions until she heard hushed whispers that made the hairs on her neck stand up and her heart rate increase. Saleem and Rahim's voices were low behind the partially cracked door. Everything told her to keep walking, but hearing her name mumbled made her stay put.

"And if Amira finds out?" Rahim questioned.

"There's nothing to find out. It ain't that deep, bruh," Saleem replied, his tone low and defensive. "I cut Brandi off the second me and Amira reconnected."

Amira froze, her mouth dropping open at the name. *Brandi?* she thought, and then it hit her. She was the same girl from his college study sessions.

"Not that deep? Brandi was blowing your phone up for weeks, bro. Calling me on social media and all types of crazy shit looking for you," Rahim spat. "And you think Amira wouldn't care about that? You trippin'."

Saleem sighed, and Amira heard the weariness in it. "What was I supposed to say, Rah? Tell her the chick I was fucking on and stringing along for years still has a thing for me even though I cut her off? It didn't feel necessary."

"Not necessary is crazy, but a'ight." Rahim's tone sounded defeated. "You really think she wouldn't care about that? You've been back with Amira for months now and you haven't said a word? That girl deserves to know the whole picture, especially now that she's your wife."

Amira's stomach twisted. She pressed a hand against the wall, trying to steady herself as the words sank in. *Was Brandi still around when we got back together? And he didn't think I needed to know?*

"It's gon' fuck things up. I know it is," Saleem admitted, his voice quieter now. "Amira was already hesitant about giving us another chance. Adding unnecessary drama was gon' have her ass running away."

Rahim let out a dry laugh. "You mean you didn't want to have the tough conversation about a past bitch, who means nothing to you. Got it, bro. I know you love her and want to protect what y'all got, but hiding stuff like this ain't the move. Amira's solid, but she's not gon' appreciate being blindsided if something pops off. I know that for a fact."

Amira backed away from the door, her heart pounding. A part of her wanted to storm in and confront him, but another part, the bigger and louder part, told her to pause. She needed a minute to process what she'd just heard.

She slipped quietly down the hall, locating the bathroom that she was supposed to be in, to begin with. Stepping inside, she closed the door behind her, leaning against it as her mind raced.

Why didn't he tell me? she thought.

It wasn't just about Brandi. Amira trusted Saleem. She believed him when he said he was all in with her. But now, this shit felt like a slap in the face and a crack in their foundation she thought was solid until now. If he'd kept this from her, what else hadn't he said?

Disappointment settled heavily in her chest. Saleem had always been the one person she thought she could be completely transparent with, the one who'd never make her question where she stood. But right now, she couldn't help but feel like she'd been left in the dark. Like all the time they spent over the months meant nothing.

Her phone vibrated in her hand, pulling her out of her thoughts. The screen lit up with a text from Saleem.

> Did you get lost? You been missing for a minute.

She stared at the message, her emotions swirling between anger and sadness. She wanted to ask him right then and there, to make him explain why he'd been sneaky. But the knot in her chest told her it wasn't a conversation meant to be had through text messages or even one for tonight. She chuckled, knowing Saleem had no clue how missing she was about to go.

Amira locked her phone and proceeded to use the bathroom. She loved Saleem, no question about it, but love didn't erase the sting of disappointment. Now, she had to decide how to approach this because no matter how much she cared for him, she couldn't let this slide. They had promised each other honesty, and right now, she wasn't sure if that promise held any weight.

"IT'S ME I DON'T TRUST."

TEN

"Girl! Why didn't nobody tell me it was this late," Jazmine groaned as they walked out of the karaoke bar and grill.

Amira could only chuckle. The drinks in her system had her feeling lovely. "I told you the time when you got up there to sing Toni Braxton. You did a horrible fucking job, by the way."

Quinn snorted. "Not you just telling her but was in there cheering her on."

"We listen, and we don't embarrass each other in front of strangers." Amira laughed. "Only we can clown her."

Jazmine sucked her teeth. "Girl, whatever. I could've been at home laid up with my man if I knew I was gon' get hated on all night. I received a standing ovation."

"They were telling you to leave," Quinn said slowly.

Amira bent over, laughing, and almost fell when Jazmine pushed her. Hurriedly, she gripped her arm. "Damn! Knock me over then."

Laughing, Jazmine said, "My bad. But, whatever. I've been kicked out of better places."

"That's right, friend. Let them know!" Amira shouted, getting looks from people in the parking lot, but they minded their business.

She felt *good*. Springtime nights in the city were always such a vibe. It wasn't too cold or too hot, and people acted like they had some sense. While her initial plans were to hang with Leerah, Sovanna, and some of their other friends at a hookah lounge down the way, Amira declined once she found out who all was going.

It was a mutual understanding in friendships that just because someone is your friend, it doesn't make them your friends' friend. And neither does their business. That was the reason Amira had kept her and Saleem's marriage private. As soon as someone thinks they have the drop about someone's life, they start running their mouth.

Leerah's friend, Nae, just so happened to be the culprit, and Amira wasn't fucking with her. According to Jazmine, who wanted to confront her, Nae was cool with Brandi. Word had gotten around about Saleem being married, and since he hadn't wifed her, Brandi decided to tell folks that their marriage was fake. Those folks were Nae, who said something along the lines of, *You sure Saleem is married?* to Leerah and Sovanna.

He was, so speaking on her husband and their marriage had Amira putting some distance between them until everyone's intentions were clear. She didn't think Leerah or Sovanna had said anything ill about her, but it was the principle. Nae shouldn't have even felt comfortable bringing Saleem's name up to them, especially regarding a woman who wasn't his wife. Fake or not.

Amira had gotten all of this information throughout the week, and Saleem had yet to say anything. She was playing it cool around the house, giving him ample space to confess that the bitch, Brandi, was still coo-coo over him and acting like a stalker, but he hadn't. Thankfully, she'd started her cycle the night they left his parents' house, so he'd been sleeping in the guest room to give her space. That was exactly what Amira needed and possibly another man since the one she had, wanted to act up.

"The men are out tonight, honey," Quinn said, eyeing the parking lot. "Look at Lucci's fine thuggin' ass."

"Mira, he and Saleem could be cousins. They look alike," Jazmine noted.

Amira locked eyes on the fine, caramel skin man with a wavy Caesar cut and juicy ass lips. She remembered when he had a head full of hair that drove the women wild. Young and old alike. He was tall like Amira liked them, too, but she was married and had heard nothing but good things about him that would surely bring her trouble. She had enough going on in her life, but it didn't hurt to play a little bit.

"Mhm. They do," Amira said, catching his gaze.

Lucci tossed her a head nod and a small grin. Amira didn't smile back. She just held eye contact. She was just the type of woman a nigga like Lucci loved to chase. Mean and off-limits. When he leaned over and said something to the even finer nigga beside him before walking her way, Amira tried to keep her cool.

"Yeah, Enzo knew to stay his ass right where he belongs." Quinn laughed.

"His wife is a straight shooter. I ain't even know he was standing there. He's invisible to me." Jazmine cackled.

Lucci's scent greeted them before he did. "What's up, pretty?" he addressed Amira first, then her girls. "Ladies."

"Don't come over here on no bullshit, Lucci," Quinn warned.

He wasn't trying to be on that at all. Only on Amira, who still hadn't cracked a grin at him.

"Me on bullshit? Never that," he said smoothly, his gaze never straying from Amira. "Just came to give Ms. Pretty some of my attention."

Amira tilted her head, studying Lucci as he stood before with a cocky grin. If he wanted to see her smile, he was going to have to work for it.

"You ain't gotta smile," he said, then leaned in for his words to only grace her ears. "But you could tell me your name. Or if you too good for that, slide me your number, and we can go from there. I'd give you mine first, but you look like the type who'd play on my phone."

Amira cracked at that. Chuckling, she said, "I'm too grown to play on people's phones."

"Not people. Just mine," Lucci said. "I wouldn't even block you."

Adjusting her purse strap on her shoulder, Amira ignored the vibrations coming from her phone. Lucci damn near stumbled backward when he saw the rock on her hand.

"Gotdamn, baby. You married?" he questioned, hoping she said no, but he knew better. Amira was looking too right not to have been someone's wife.

"Yes, she is," Jazmine answered for her.

Lucci licked his lips. "Even better. That means we can sneak for however long you need to. No commitments."

"You're bold, huh?" Amira asked.

"When I need to be. You like that?"

Before she could respond and tell him no, the sound of a roaring engine ended their conversation, catching everyone's attention. Heads turned as a sleek, smoky grey Maserati MC20 whipped into the parking lot, backing into a spot directly across from its intended target with precision as if they owned the lot. And he did. Amira's stomach did that stupid flip when the door lifted, and Saleem's tall frame stepped out. His black jogger set and skully on his head were the perfect fit for the occasion.

"Oh, bitch. It's a wraaaaap," Jazmine sang, doing Mariah Carey no justice.

Saleem didn't bother to lower his door or turn off

the engine. Instead, with a commanding presence, he swaggered to the hood and sat down. This move alone shifted the atmosphere. It got eerily quiet, or at least that's how Amira felt.

Saleem stretched his long legs, planted his feet firmly on the asphalt, and crossed his hands in front of him. Amira's entire world stopped spinning when they locked eyes. She looked calm on the outside, but her insides were causing a riot. Heat rushed through her face, and she shifted her weight in her heeled calf-length booties. She could barely register anything Jazmine or Quinn was saying as she tried controlling her breathing. A little playing hadn't turned out to be fun at all.

Amira's emotions were a tangled mess. Partially smug at how Lucci's flirtations suddenly felt like child's play, slightly anxious at what Saleem's sudden arrival meant, and a bit thrilled. Thrilled in a way that made her want to smile, but she forced herself to keep it together.

Amira's breath hitched when Saleem reached into the pocket of his jacket. Then, it settled when she saw he'd grabbed his phone. It accelerated again when he placed it to his ear, and her phone vibrated inside her purse. She rushed to clumsily grab it, thanks to the roller coaster of emotions he'd just taken her heart through. There weren't even any seatbelts on this ride.

Saleem had her at the top when she swiped the screen to answer his call. Amira didn't speak. She didn't have to.

"If I have to come over there and get that nigga out of your face, we gon' have to arrange conjugal visits or go on the run. Choose one."

Amira jumped off the ride.

Fuck falling.

She pushed past Lucci, who was shaking his head, not knowing he was a second away from no longer having one. Behind his wife, if a woman ever took him seriously, he'd lay an army down behind her, so he understood it. Clearly not enough, though.

All eyes were on Amira as her heels clicked softly with determined steps across the parking lot. She kept her chin high and eyes forward. Her fitted Bermuda shorts hugged her curves just right, while a sliver of her stomach was exposed in the off-the-shoulder cropped top. Her skin tingled the closer she got to him. Saleem's eyes trailed down her frame and back up, before lingering on her face. His jaw flexed when Amira got close enough for him to see the faint smirk playing on her lips. She knew exactly what she was doing.

While she called herself putting on a show, a car speeding through the parking lot did the same. Amira's head snapped in its direction, and her body froze for a split second. She hadn't registered how fast or how close the car was until tires screeched against the pavement. Jazmine and Quinn hollered behind her, their voices all a panic blur.

Before she could process what was happening, Saleem yanked her to him and into the air before they stumbled backward. Amira felt like the wind had gotten knocked out of her. Her head spun for a moment before she steadied in his arms. The Challenger zoomed past, getting shouted at and chased down by a few people standing around. The air filled with the smell of burnt rubber as they peeled out of the parking lot, and Amira's heart pounded so hard she felt it in her ears.

Saleem held her tightly against his chest, his heart in his feet, spilling out against the same pavement. All signs of life flashed before his eyes at that moment. Whatever he was about to say once she made it to him didn't even matter. The thought of losing her that quickly made him want to throw up, then find the driver of the vehicle to teach him some parking lot etiquette or size him for a casket. Nothing but dangerous thoughts filled his mind when it came to Amira being harmed.

"You okay," he soothed, rubbing her back. "I got you."

Amira was trembling as her hands gripped the front of his jacket. Her legs wobbled as she blinked up at him, still trying to catch her breath. Saleem was breathing so hard, his breaths were audible. His arms stayed wrapped around her. One hand rested protectively on her back while the other cradled her head as if making sure she was still there. Amira swallowed hard as Jazmine and Quinn ran over to her.

"That was... oh my God." She sniffled, shaken up so badly, that words struggled to form in her brain.

Thankful, Saleem closed his eyes briefly at the sound of her voice, and they popped back open when she wiggled out of his embrace. His brow furrowed.

"Where you going?" he asked, tone strangled with utter confusion.

"You... I. I was walking over here because you told me to, and—" Amira didn't finish her sentence, just shook her head.

She pulled away from him, and Saleem snatched

her back, placing her in a bear hug. "Don't do that," he said with an even tone directly in her ear, laced with something that sent a shiver down Amira's spine. "Don't give these mothafuckas something to talk about. Let's get in the car and go home."

Amira bit into her bottom lip. "Yeah... let's go home so I can tell you about yourself and that bitch, Brandi, since you failed to do so!" she spat.

Saleem's top lip curled as he leaned away to look into her eyes. "Do you think I give a fuck about another woman when I *literally* just almost lost you?"

"I don't know who or what you care about anymore," she insulted.

The disgust in her voice was just as sickening as her expression. That was a low blow, and Saleem felt the punch everywhere. Amira could've just pushed him off the ride when she jumped earlier to prove a point. Saleem was sure the fall would've caused less damage.

"Nah," he grumbled, not giving a fuck about the people staring at them. "How can you even fix your mouth to say that to me? I fucking love you. You're my wife!" he fumed.

"Act like it then!"

Her bellow shook Saleem's core. It rocked and

split the very foundation he thought he'd built to last. Angry tears threatened to spill from Amira's eyes, but she didn't allow them to. Not while they were out here in the open. She wouldn't dare. They'd already performed enough for the night.

Saleem stood there for a beat, his chest rising and falling with restrained fury as he stared at Amira. Her words cut deep, and he saw the pain behind her anger, but it didn't make him hurt any less. Without another word, he shuffled her to the passenger side and opened the door. Amira stood there, contemplating her next move but knew she had to be a woman. *This* was marriage. She couldn't just run away like she was used to.

"Get in." Saleem's voice was low and steady.

Amira didn't even argue. She was too drained to put up another fight. When she flopped down, Saleem reached across her chest and buckled her in before closing the door and making his way to the driver's seat.

The ride home was quick and silent. Amira sat stiffly, her arms crossed as she stared out the window. She felt his frustration radiating off him, but she wasn't about to break the silence first. She was saving all her energy for when they got inside. If he wanted to talk, it was best he speak up.

Saleem was fighting to keep his cool. Her words replayed in his mind like a broken record, each repetition hitting harder than the last. He gripped the wheel tighter, wondering how this stupid situation, which could've been avoided, was their first real dispute. Of all things... it stemmed from a woman letting a man do as he pleased, whereas Amira wasn't letting a damn thing slide. She'd end this mutually beneficial agreement, pack a bag, and stay at a hotel before she *ever* let him embarrass her.

When they pulled up to the house, Saleem turned off the car but didn't move to get out. Instead, he leaned back in his seat, exhaling heavily as he ran a hand down his face. Amira reached for the door handle, but his voice stopped her.

"Don't."

Amira froze, her hand hovering in the air before she let it drop back into her lap. She turned to face him with a guarded expression. "Don't what?"

Saleem sighed, clicking on the dome light. "C'mon, baby. Don't try and get out like we don't have anything to talk about. That shit..." He paused. His voice was firm but wasn't loud.

Raising his voice wouldn't get the message across any clearer, although he'd heard hers loud and crystal clear about acting like she was his wife. He didn't want them to act anymore. Saleem hadn't from the jump, and he thought they'd established that this thing between them was more than a favor. It was beyond keeping a roof over Amira's head and showing Youssef that he wasn't less of a man.

Saleem's eyes bore into hers, and Amira saw something other than the anger she was expecting. She saw unspoken pain. Not because he was hurting but because he'd hurt her.

Amira swallowed hard, her defenses faltering. "Saleem..."

"No," he cut her off, turning as much as he could in his seat to face her fully. "You said I act like I don't love you. That's what you think?"

Her throat tightened, and she blinked rapidly to keep her tears at bay. "I don't know what to think anymore. I used to believe your words were bond, but... I heard you that day at your parents' house. The things you told Rahim. Those aren't the actions of a man who claimed he'd protect me."

"That was a fact," Saleem said through gritted teeth. "I will."

"Keeping me in the dark in this marriage isn't protection... it's control disguised as care. You can't withhold information from me because you think

I'll leave. You still don't trust me to stay when shit gets rough?"

The quake in her voice made Saleem squeeze his eyes shut. It wasn't that he didn't trust her. It was the fact that every time he looked at Amira, he saw everything he stood to lose if he messed this up. He wasn't prepared to do life without her again. So, he'd chosen deafening silence over honesty, believing it was the safest route. Keeping her away from the bullshit to protect them and her mental was a risk Saleem didn't know would cost him so much.

His eyes softened when he reopened them, and Saleem reached for her hand, smiling inside when he felt the cold diamond grace his skin. She didn't pull away this time. Instead, Amira gave him the space he'd given her all week to clear the air.

"It's me I don't trust, but I'm trying, baby."

His raw vulnerability made Amira want to hold him. It caught her off guard, and she realized how much weight he'd been carrying, thinking she'd leave at the first sign of trouble. That...made her sad and sorry, too.

"I'm trying to figure this husband thing out without losing you for good. I can't let that happen," he said, shaking his head.

A tear slipped down her cheek before she could stop it, and she squeezed his hand.

"You're not going to lose me," she whispered, her voice trembling.

"Then stop tryna push me away, a'ight," he murmured, leaning closer. Saleem couldn't help but kiss her lips. "I'm sorry for not telling you about Brandi and the weird shit she was on. She'd never been an issue until she found out you were my wife."

Amira smirked. "Hoes real tender about my title."

"Good. That bitch can fall off the bone for all I care."

Amira choked on a laugh. Her body bounced as she cracked up laughing, not believing he'd just said that. What made the moment even more hilarious was knowing he meant that shit with everything in him. Saleem didn't typically call women out of their name, but Brandi had pissed him off. She was going to be whomever the hell he felt like, which was nobody.

She'd been a placeholder in his life the second she found out he and Amira were no longer together. Saleem should've known then that she wasn't worth his time because the woman meant for him would never settle for second best or let him treat her as such.

Amira had done neither, and that's why she had his last name and was about to live the best life Saleem could give her.

He frowned. "What? She can. I'm not about to play with her ass or anyone else when it comes to you. I'll hurt a hoe's feelings and make her wish she never met me for trying to create friction between us. Nah. I ain't going for it."

Amira rubbed his hand. "I know you're not, and that's why I love you." She kissed his cheek and pulled back when it flexed underneath her lips. "What's wrong?"

Gently, he gripped her chin. "Did you have fun tonight?"

A range of answers and emotions flashed through her eyes. Amira had gone from listening to Jazmine's horrible singing to playing with Lucci's life, almost losing hers, and now was sitting in the car having a heart-to-heart conversation with her husband... a man she'd been in love with since she was eighteen. Fun? Her night had been fucking insane!

"Um... yeah. Sure."

"That's good, Angel..." he said, caressing her

cheek with the pad of his thumb before slowly dragging it across her bottom lip. "When we get in this house, I'ma show you just how much more fun you could've had with me if you had answered your phone."

Amira gulped and nodded, not knowing she was agreeing to see a side of Saleem that would bring the crazy out of her. At least he'd given her a heads-up.

If placing blindfolds over her eyes and denying her orgasms was what Saleem considered fun, Amira wouldn't even hang up the phone once he called. They could talk all day long. It'd been thirty-seven minutes of foreplay, and Amira was on the verge of crying because she wanted to cum so badly.

She laid naked on their bed, legs spread wide, thighs and wrists bound, completely open for him. The padded restraints around her wrists, straps around her thighs, and cushioned neck strap were comfortable and beginner-friendly enough for Saleem to have his fun. This was for her enjoyment, too, and she'd surrendered complete control.

Walking toward the edge of the bed without a stitch of clothing on, Saleem dragged his hand down her propped leg, trailing fingertips over her ankle.

The thigh straps elevated her knees in the air. She could wiggle her legs a bit, but not much.

"How many times did I call you tonight, Angel?"

It'd been a few minutes since he allowed her to hear his voice, so Amira's chest heaved at the sudden deepness. Every nerve ending was heightened, with her vision restricted. Increased awareness of where he stood made her anticipate his next move even more.

Amira blinked rapidly behind the darkness, trying to recall how many times her phone had vibrated throughout the night. She remembered the first two, but after her second drink, she had no idea. When she heard the buzz from the vibrator begin, she squirmed along the sheets. Punishment for taking too long was his favorite.

"Baby... wait. Wait. Okay...I was going to answer yooooou. *Uhhhnn!*"

Saleem wasted no time applying the suction over her engorged clit. He held it in place and bit into his bottom lip.

"How many times?" Saleem asked, pinching her nipples.

Her head thrashed against the pillow, knowing if she said the wrong number, he'd just start over. Placing his mouth over her sensitive peaks, Saleem swirled his tongue over them before pulling away. Seeing her legs shake, he removed the vibrator and just held it. If her eyes were open, Amira would've been seeing red she was so pissed.

"Ohhh my gosh! Please, please!"

He placed it back over her clit and held it in place while stroking his dick. Since she wanted to play with his feelings tonight, he had to show her how competitive things could get. Flirting with another nigga, not answering his calls, and hollering at him weren't things his wife did. Nah, not her.

"Saleem," she said, her voice trembling. "I can't... I can't, baby. Please."

Not wanting her to pass out, he removed the toy, giving her a second to breathe. Amira's chest heaved, and her body was slick with sweat. Reaching toward the nightstand, he grabbed the white towel from a bowl of ice water and wrung it out. Gently, he patted her forehead before trailing it across her titties and down the center of her chest.

Tossing it to the side, he counted down from sixty before saying, "If you guess correctly, I'll let you cum."

"Five," she blubbered.

Saleem made a *tsk* sound with his mouth. "Wrong answer."

She whined to the point of tears. They slid down the sides of her face into her ears. Instead of using the toy, Saleem held the button to power it off and lowered his head between her legs. His tongue made slow, torturous licks from the top to the bottom, not missing a drop. He slid two fingers inside her, barely needing to move them because she was so aroused. She pulsed from the stimulation alone.

Her moans grew louder, and her body trembled as Saleem delivered rapid flicks. Back and forth, he didn't ease up. She was breathing hard and fast, matching the rhythm of his tongue. Saleem relished in the taste of her, sucking her clit gently, then with an intensity that made Amira's stomach cave. She screamed so loud when Saleem removed his mouth and chuckled lowly.

"I haaaate you!" she cried, writhing against the bed.

He smirked, rubbing her thighs. "It's okay. I love you too, baby. We can end this if you tell me what I want to hear."

Amira sniffled. Her fucking nose was running worse than her pussy. Breathing harshly, she blinked behind the satin material.

"Can you...I want to see," she requested once she caught her breath.

Without hesitation, Saleem slid the material off her face. She squeezed her lids together, then opened her eyes, wishing she could rub them. Saleem ran a hand down her neck and held her there, staring like she was the most beautiful woman he had ever seen. Amira didn't even care about how fine he was, hovering over her with pure, unadulterated lust and love in his copper eyes. She was exhausted.

"You tired?" he asked, reading her mind.

Her lip poked out as she weakly nodded. Saleem kissed her and leaned back to position himself perfectly between her legs. On his knees, he dragged the underside of his dick down her slickness. Sliding the tip against her lips, he stared her in the eyes.

"I'll give you a hint," he said, patting his heaviness against wet skin.

"Mmm," Amira moaned. "O...Okay."

Licking his lips, Saleem hoped she could read his mind because he was so ready to slide in her, goosebumps coated his hairy arms.

"The number of times I called you tonight is on the inside of your ring."

Her brows dented, and her head slowly turned to the left. She eyed the custom flawless white diamond oval cut ring designed by Naaz, the jeweler.

The inside of her ring was engraved with Saleem's name, the month, day, and last two digits of the year they met. She knew the number of carats was the month and day but wasn't sure if that's how many calls of his she'd missed. Amira rolled the numbers around in her discombobulated brain as he continued to toy with her clit, dipping the head of his dick slightly inside her. Saleem had been disciplined all night; a lil' sample was rightfully deserved.

"Um," Amira hesitated, licking her dry lips.

She knew the day they met. It had been scribbled on notebook paper while she zoned out in class with hearts circling it. It was even the passcode to her phone at a point in time. Saleem pressed his tip harder into her clit, giving her just the encouragement she needed.

"Ten?" she asked, praying to God she was right.

Saleem smiled, and she could've cried. Leaning forward, he said, "There you go, baby. Now, cum on this dick, and never play with your husband again."

3/8/10 – the day that they met.

3.8 – the number of carats sitting on her finger.

10 – the number of times Saleem called her phone tonight.

. . .

He'd played a straight mind fuck game, but it was all worth it once he slid inside of her. The throaty groan he released while sliding into her was all Amira needed to climax. Her body convulsed before Saleem could even get five strokes in. He'd given her exactly what she was craving. Stars danced behind her lids as he pumped into her.

"Uuuh, I love you!" Amira moaned, saying exactly what Saleem wanted to hear, to have him blasting off inside of her.

He grunted and kissed her neck. "I love you more, Mrs. Majid. And you better never forget that."

"LET THEM KNOW YOUR HUSBAND HAS YOUR BACK."

ELEVEN

Amira hadn't moved from the bed in two days. She couldn't move. Saleem ran her a bath with Epsom salt for two days straight, massaged her body down, and tried his best to be gentle while sliding into her from the side this morning, but that wasn't enough. Amira was exhausted but thoroughly satisfied. She'd been in and out of her sleep all day and had no plans to get up unless it was to empty her bladder.

She was deliciously sore and wasn't complaining, and she now knew to never play with her man. If he wanted to teach her a lesson, it'd been learned. Smiling at the memory, Amira yawned and stretched her body across the bed. She had it all to herself right now, and it felt good to sprawl out.

"Mmm," she groaned, popping her neck and scratching her left boob.

Nothing compared to lying in the nude with the fan on, having no plans. Calling off of work had been worth it.

She was just about to snuggle back under the covers when her phone rang. It was on the nightstand since she didn't even have enough energy to be on it. Knowing that it couldn't have been Saleem since he was downstairs, but also wondering if he was testing her, she reached over to grab it. She'd be damned if he gave her a repeat of the night before when she was still recovering. He had the nerve to hold her hand and say his prayers aloud this morning, then roll over and slide his dick into her like he'd just blessed a meal. Amira was already thinking of ways to hide from him, but it wouldn't be necessary because it wasn't Saleem calling.

It was her auntie, Sonya. Seeing her name wasn't unusual, but Amira immediately got a feeling that whatever she was calling for wouldn't be good. Sighing, she answered and placed the call on speaker.

"Hey, Auntie," she said.

"Hey, Mira, girl," Sonya said cheerfully. "What you got going on?"

Amira smiled, hearing her voice. It'd been a while. Though she and Quinn were close, they had ongoing issues with their parents, and Amira stayed out of their drama unless Quinn asked for her advice. Still, there was no love lost.

"Not much. Just relaxing," Amira said. "What you doing?"

"Over here washing a load of clothes. Something told me I needed to call and check on you. I'd been meaning to, anyway. Congratulations!"

"Thank you," Amira said solemnly, not even finding the need to ask what she was congratulating her for.

Of course, she knows I'm married, she thought.

"Oh, hold on now. Why you gotta sound like that with me?" Sonya asked.

"Like what?"

"Like I was the one you cut off," she said matter-of-factly. "I ain't your mama and ain't did nothing to you."

"Okay, Auntie, anything else?" Amira said smartly, ready to hang up in her face.

"Girl!" Sonya shouted. "What the hell has gotten into you? First, you up and move in with some man, and then you go and marry him without telling anybody. Oh, but Quinn was there. Mmhm. I saw her looking at the pictures of y'all the other day."

Amira laughed. "I hope you liked them."

"I did, actually," Sonya said, her voice softening, and Amira's heart did the same.

She wasn't trying to take it there with her, but she'd started with her first. Sonya knew how defensive she and Evelyn had made her, yet they acted surprised when she showed them the same energy they had given her.

"Thank you," Amira mumbled.

"Mmhm, you're welcome. I just don't get it, niece. You really hurt Evelyn by cutting her off. She's still your mama."

"And I'm still her daughter that she carried for ten months, but does she act like it? No."

Sonya sighed. "I get it. But no matter what happened between you two, you can't—"

"Auntie...please stop. Okay?" Amira cut in, her voice firm and unwavering. "I've set my boundaries with your sister and if you want to keep any type of relationship with me, please don't bring her up in any capacity."

"Boundaries?" Sonya scoffed. "She's your blood, Mira. And she's hurting just like I know you are."

"I no longer allow her or anything associated

with her to stir my emotions. Neither should you. You and I both know how she is, but you choose to turn a blind eye because she's your sister. I'm not. She made her choices, and I made mine. I don't owe her anything after all the trauma she's caused me," Amira said, feeling a lump rise in her throat.

She swallowed it down, refusing to let Evelyn pull those emotions out of her again.

Sonya sighed dramatically. "I just don't know how you can say that. So, you're never going to talk to her again?"

"Will Barack Obama ever be president again?" Amira asked slickly, not giving Sonya a chance to answer. "Exactly. It's okay to outgrow people. I've come to terms with that."

"Girl." Sonya laughed in disbelief. "She's your mother."

"And she's a person just like me. I'm not about to sit on this phone and go back and forth about my feelings. So, thank you for congratulating me, but I'm done with this. If and when you decide to call me again, please do not bring up your sister, or it'll be the last time we speak."

With that, Amira hung up the phone and tossed the covers off her legs. Sonya was probably over there calling her every name except the one her sister gave her, and Amira didn't care. It baffled Amira at how selfish some people could be. Sonya was basically telling Amira that since she put up with Evelyn's mess, she had to as well, and it would never happen.

Call her stubborn or anything else; it wouldn't make her change the relationship she no longer had or was interested in rekindling with Evelyn. It was what it was, and that was the sad truth.

Forcing herself to get up and not fall into a sadness over something she'd made terms with, Amira climbed from the bed. She stepped inside the bathroom, and the automatic lights came on, illuminating the space and brightening her mood. Pulling the glass door open to their massive shower, she stepped inside and twisted the knobs to the far right. She wanted it hot as possible. While it reached the temperature of her liking, she sat on the toilet to pee.

The second she closed her eyes, thinking she was about to take a relaxing piss to herself, she heard Saleem's deep voice singing a song she just knew he had to go to YouTube to play. *If I Had You* by Frankie floated from his lips as if he'd written the song himself. When he tried hitting a high note, Amira snickered. Her body began to sway on its own to one of the smoothest songs, in her opinion, that came out in the nineties.

"Angel, if I had yooou," Saleem sang, sounding closer to the bathroom.

Amira stayed seated and smirked when he stepped inside, hitting a sexy two-step and snapping his fingers. She giggled, and he grinned wide before pausing the song. Giving her no personal space, Saleem walked over to her and kissed her lips that she didn't hesitate to pucker.

"Bae, what you doing?" he asked.

Amira looked down at her naked frame, glanced toward the running shower, and back at him, then blinked twice. Saleem chuckled.

"Awww shit. You in one of your moods. Let me leave you alone," he said, and she smirked.

"I mean... I thought it was obvious," she said.

"I should've asked what you were about to do. Aye," he said, lifting her face to him. "What's the matter?"

Her eyes watered, and she shook her head. "Nothing."

Saleem lifted his brow, and she sighed.

"I just got off the phone with my Auntie Sonya, and she irritated me by bringing up my mama."

Rubbing her cheek, Saleem said, "Yeah, gon'

head and block her, too. Didn't you already tell her what was up between y'all?"

Amira nodded. "Yes. I guess she thought something would change."

"Nah. The only thing that's 'bout to change around this bitch is your number. What's wrong with people, man?"

Seeing him just as upset as she was made Amira love him more. Knowing he would go to bat for her with anyone and carry the emotional weight with her so she didn't have to carry it alone, had her silently thanking God in her head. It was one thing to take care of her physically, but that emotional and mental care hit different on so many levels. Amira now fully understood where he was coming from with the Brandi situation.

Amira stood up after wiping herself, flushed the toilet, and washed her hands at the sink. Saleem sat on the upholstered cream ottoman in the middle of the floor and watched her through the mirror. Seeing her in a foul mood had him pissed, but he knew staying upset would only make her madder, so he tried to relax.

"You know you don't have to explain yourself to anyone, right?" he asked softly, though his jaw flexed. Amira nodded. "You made boundaries for a reason. Mothafuckas better fall in line 'cause the last thing I'ma let you do is feel guilty for protecting your peace. Fuck them, a'ight?"

She blinked away tears. "Okay."

"And if Quinn gotta problem with you cutting her mama off, she can get blocked too."

Amira chuckled. "Now... how'd she get in this? Quinn will forever have my back and ride for me."

Saleem shrugged. "Shit, I'm just saying. Everybody can get ghost. Let them know your husband has your back one hundred and ten percent and *will* spin some shit 'bout you. Riding ain't enough."

Smirking, Amira stepped away from the counter. "I like that in you, baby, 'cause so will I when it comes to you. You my twin." She chuckled.

Saleem heard what she said, but the way her titties were sitting heavy and nipples poking, that's all he saw.

"Yeah, and these pretty ass titties right here are my favorite twins," he said, cupping her titties in both hands before sloshing his tongue over them.

Amira instantly pushed his head away. "No. Hell no," she fussed. "My girl is still down there aching."

Saleem drew his head back, smirking, sucking his teeth. "You so dramatic." He laughed. "I just wanted to lick on em' a lil bit."

"You wanna lick something? There's a brand new box of popsicles in the freezer," Amira said, laughing. "Ordered them earlier when you went to the gym."

All laughter ceased when Saleem lowered his sweats and briefs to the heated tile floor. He stroked his dick, base to pretty two-toned hued tip, watching Amira damn near slobber on herself.

"Your pussy hurting, but your mouth not," Saleem said huskily.

When she smirked, Saleem wanted to clap his hands. Walking over to him, Amira pushed his hand away and stroked him. Pressing her boobs into his chest, she puckered her lips for a kiss that he gave before she lowered her head and licked his nipples.

"Sss," Saleem hissed at the sensation.

Walking backward with him still in her hand, Amira sat on the ottoman and licked the precum pebbled at the tip. Nastily, she spat on it before covering him with her mouth. Her head bobbed as she used one hand to stroke his length. When she let him touch the back of her throat and gag on it, Saleem gripped her hair.

"Gotdamn!" he spat, placing the other hand on her head.

Amira's eyes lit up, and he caught on immediately. She widened her mouth as he widened his stance. Seeing the pleasure on his face as he fucked her mouth made Amira so happy to please him. He deserved this, plus more.

"You taste so good, baby," she praised, then sucked him back into her wet mouth.

Saleem's nostrils flared as she got disgusting with it, just how he liked. Amira's eyes watered, and the erotic noises echoing around them, especially Saleem's grunts, had her propping one leg up and rubbing her pussy.

"Mmmm," Saleem groaned, his toes popping. "Yeah, that's... it. You playing with my pussy?"

She nodded on the dick, and his eyes dropped between her legs. Wet thighs greeted him. He licked his lips.

"Switch hands. Let me see that ring on your finger while you cum," Saleem instructed.

Amira switched hands, and Saleem almost nutted down her throat. Knowing she was his and loved him for who he was gave him a feeling like no other. When Amira massaged his balls with her free hand and hollowed her jaws, Saleem's back stiffened.

"You gon' make me nut all in your pretty ass

mouth," he gritted through clenched teeth, pumping his hips.

Amira pulled off of him with a popping noise to quickly say, "Do it."

He was right back inside her mouth and releasing his seeds ten seconds later. Saleem pulled out some after she'd swallowed most of it down her throat and spurted the last bits on the lower half of her face. Smearing him into her lips, his chest heaved at how pretty she still looked with him all over her. Amira smiled, not realizing how much she enjoyed being degraded in such a way. Only her husband could bring that freak up out of her.

"Mmm hmm," she hummed, licking her lips, using her index finger to wipe and swallow the rest. Saleem's diet was so clean that Amira could do this all day. With his eyes fluttering, Saleem backed away from her.

"What kind of car you want?" he blurted.

Amira's face screwed up, and she chuckled. "Huh?"

"We're going to the dealership once we get out of the shower."

She was sure she'd suck the thoughts out of him because he wasn't making any sense.

"I don't need a new car, though."

"But I'm buying you one. That's what I came up here to tell you, then I got sidetracked. You be fucking me up, Angel," he said teasingly as if he hadn't come bothering her.

Amira smiled. "Any kind?"

"You want a spaceship? You can get whatever with the way you just clowned on this dick. I can't even see straight," he claimed, wiping his eyes.

Giggling, Amira stood up. Stepping his way, she puckered her lips, and like the lovingly-nasty nigga he was, Saleem tongued her down. Amira whimpered when he smacked her ass before breaking their kiss.

"You'd look good in a Range Rover."

Amira shook her head. "Uuum. I was thinking more along the lines of a BMW. The X6 with red seats."

Saleem smirked. "You naming all that like you didn't just say *I don't need a new car*, though," he mocked, making her laugh.

"I never said I wasn't looking, pooh. Your wife will take that and some food. Thank you," she said, turning to get in the shower, which she had forgotten all about.

Rushing behind her, Saleem wrapped her in a

hug and nuzzled her neck as she laughed from the tickling sensation. "Say it again. My what?"

"Your wife," Amira sang, giggling harder.

"Yeah... that's what I like to hear, baby. My wife can get whatever she wants."

While she thought she'd be grieving the relationships of one or possibly two people in her life, Saleem had saved the day, making her forget why she was sad in the first place.

"WAS THIS ALL FOR YOU TO GET BACK
AT ME?"

TWELVE

No matter how busy his schedule was, Saleem always made time to hit the gym. Besides keeping him in shape, he enjoyed the mental freedom it gave him. Some days, he'd been in there for hours and not even realize it. After hitting his last rep, Saleem cleaned the station off, chugged his water down, and glanced around the room. His boys, Cree and Synovi, stood by the exit doors, preparing to leave. They'd all gotten there around the same time. Grabbing his bag off the floor, he snagged his towel and wiped his face before heading their way.

Saleem caught up to them after speaking to someone he knew. Pushing through the doors, he sighed with appreciation at the coolness in the air.

He didn't know when May decided to become a summer month, but it'd been hot the last few days, and he wasn't feeling it. Walking behind the duo, Saleem shook his head at them going back and forth already.

"I'm just saying," Synovi started, his tone so chill, "if we're being honest, I had the most reps tonight."

Saleem snorted, shaking his head as he made it to his SUV. "I'm not getting in the middle of that. *But* since we're keeping it real, Cree did clown you on the bench press."

Cree smirked, clapping Synovi on the back. "You hear that? Ain't no way you're out lifting me, bro. Just stick to those baby weights you love so much."

Synovi pushed his hand away. "Yeah, a'ight. You the same nigga thinking he still got it 'cause you ran track in college. Hang it up, cuz."

Saleem barked out a laugh. "Aye...Cree, what'd you run again?"

Cree flipped them both off, and they all laughed.

"And that's exactly why I be breaking you nigga's ankles on the court."

"Who?" Saleem said, popping his head up after tossing his bag in the passenger seat. "Them weights must have you a little light headed thinking you can run with me."

"Man, here you go." Cree laughed. "What... you wanna put some money up next game?"

"You ain't said nothing I ain't heard before," Saleem waved him off, laughing. "Every other week you be complaining about something hurting."

"Both of y'all some elders. Surprised y'all don't get social security checks," Synovi clowned. He was the youngest, but unless you knew them personally, you'd never know it. They all were successful business owners and had made a name for themselves.

"You still got Torin's titty milk on your breath. Relax," Cree said.

"My Love's titties shouldn't even be on your mind. Weird ass nigga."

Cree's body folded as he laughed. One thing Synovi didn't play about was his woman, Torin. He didn't have a smile on his face or anything.

"Yeah... you niggas is wild," Saleem said, chuckling. "Cree, you know he's sensitive."

"Go blend a smoothie or something, bitch," Synovi jested and walked off toward his Denali.

Saleem laughed loud. "Man, that nigga is petty. Ol' crybaby ass!"

Cree was still weak, wiping tears off his face. "That man told you to get in the kitchen."

"I ain't tripping. Being in that kitchen done made me millions."

Straightenening up, Cree nodded. He knew that for sure. They'd made a few together.

"Straight up. Aye, though. I been wanting to rap with you about something."

"What's up?" Saleem asked.

As a man, Cree didn't even want to bring this to him, but he'd do anything for Leerah, just like he knew Saleem would for Amira.

"Our women still ain't speaking," Cree said.

Saleem scratched his scalp. "Nah. I'ont think so."

"They aren't. Leerah snapped on me the other day when I asked if she wanted me to bring her a juice home."

Saleem drew his head back. "Damn." He chuckled. "What I do?"

"One band, one sound. You know how that goes." Cree shrugged.

"Yeah, I do. I ain't getting into that, though. My wife feels how she feels, and I don't blame her."

Cree nodded. "Respect. You know we get the rundown on shit and be lost. She mad at me 'cause I told her Nae was messy for speaking on y'all marriage."

Saleem laughed. "Bitch is messy. Next thing you know, she gon' be round here saying Lando is yours."

"He is mine," Cree said, not a hint of humor in his voice.

"Aye. I ain't mean—"

"I know," Cree said, cutting him off. "I get what you saying, though. Too much pillow talking going on. I just be trying have a peaceful night."

"Aye. We sleep good at the crib." Saleem laughed. "Ain't nobody making us lose sleep over some lies. You see what I got on," Saleem said, holding his hand up to flash his wedding band.

It was passed down to him from Youssef, and he was honored to wear it.

Cree looked down at his hand. "Might fuck around and get me one," he said seriously, and they slapped hands.

"You know Naaz gon' get you right if you on that."

Cree nodded, already putting plans in motion. "Fasho. I'm out, though. Gotta go get my youngin' from my gramps," he said, talking about his grandpa who raised him.

He and Landon had become thick as thieves and it was the cutest thing ever. They were generations apart but kicked it like best friends. Cree couldn't help but wonder what mess they'd gotten into today.

"Be safe," Saleem said, walking around to the driver's side and hopping in.

The thought of having kids hit him when he pulled out of the parking lot. Continuing his legacy had been heavy on his mind lately, and it was because he was finally with a woman worth creating a few lives with. Youssef was one hell of a father, and Saleem hoped he could be half as the man he was one day.

Needing to hear Amira's voice on his drive home, Saleem dialed her up. He couldn't help but grin as the word Wife popped up on the dash. He programmed her number under the name the day he ran into her at his Aunt Joyce's crib, already knowing she'd be his. When the phone continued to ring before going to voicemail, he frowned.

Calling it again, he received the same results. His jaw flexed, thinking about the last time he had to blow her line down. It'd been far too long since that situation occurred, so he hoped Amira wasn't playing games.

Sighing, he shook his head and ditched the plans to go the store and headed straight home instead. He wasn't trying to think the worst, but Saleem should've been. It seemed like the worst always happened to them, but nothing prepared him for what he walked in on after whipping into the driveway.

Saleem dropped his duffle bag to the ground and wanted to go with it. Amira stood there with a flushed face because she'd been crying, gripping the handle of her suitcase and holding an envelope in the other hand.

With his heart about to jump out of his chest, Saleem asked as calmly and carefully as he could, "Where you going, Angel?"

"Don't," she said, her voice cracking. She cleared her throat and pulled herself together. "Don't you stand there and call me that."

Saleem blinked, trying to figure out what he'd done wrong. "Okay... I won't call you that. What's up with the suitcase, though?"

"I'm done with this. You can have this house, the truck, the gifts, your last name. Everything. I don't want none of this shit," she seethed, then remembered something.

When she began twisting her ring off, Saleem's stomach hollowed. "Yo, what are you doing?" Saleem tried walking up to her, and she launched the ring at his chest. The clanking noise it made when it hit the ground was just as deafening as her following words that vibrated Saleem's chest.

"This was all fake!" she screamed, tears making their appearance. "You...you've been lying this entire time, and...and look at me. Fell for everything. I trusted you! I fucking trusted you, Saleem!"

"Amira, come on. I haven't lied to you about anything. I don't even know what you're talking about."

Hurriedly, she lifted the envelope in her hand. "Then what the fuck is this?"

Her tone was so cold it chilled Saleem's sweat-soaked body. Amira's hands trembled as she pulled the letter from the envelope. The papers felt like fire and needles pricking in her hands as she unfolded them.

"Oh, you can't talk now?" she taunted. "You always have soooo much to say, but now you want to be a fucking mime!" she snapped. "Speak up, nigga!"

Saleem bit the inside of his cheek to keep from talking crazy to her. "You gon' read what the papers say or not?"

Amira let out a bitter laugh, cocking her head to the side. "Oh. You wanna be funny?"

He sighed and shook his head. When he reached for them to read himself, Amira flung them in the air. Saleem glared at her with his blood boiling but kept his cool. Bending down, he grabbed the three sheets and stood straight.

"Mhm. Go ahead and read them to me!" she spat. "All this talk about your wife this, your wife that. Oh my gosh, I'm so *fucking* stupid!" she fumed.

Saleem only needed to read the first few lines of the top page to understand why she was wilding out. He didn't know if someone was trying to get buried but playing with his livelihood, claiming he'd receive an inheritance for finally being married, wasn't a joke. When his eyes lifted and Amira wiped more tears from her face, he felt like a piece of shit and hadn't even done anything to feel that way. Anger settled in his chest after seeing who signed off on the clause.

Subject: Notice of Inheritance – Conditions of Release

Dear Saleem Majid,

It is with great pleasure to inform you that the inheritance of 10.7 million dollars has successfully been wired to your trust fund account ending in 1230. Per the stipulations of your father, Youssef Majid, the inheritance has been obtained for the fulfillment of entering into a legally recognized marriage with Amira Scott.

Tossing the papers, Saleem didn't bother to read the rest. He couldn't even see straight right now.

"Baby," he said calmly, voice so heavy with emotion he could hardly get the word out. "I don't know who's playing games with us, but you know I didn't marry you for no money. Come on now."

Amira shook her head. "You're really going to stand there and act like you didn't know all this time? We just talked about you not telling me things to protect my feelings, and all this time, you were lying. How long were you going to keep me in the blind this time? Just tell the truth."

"I am!" he shouted, and she flinched. Saleem squeezed his eyes shut, water pooling in them when he reopened them.

"I'ma just leave before... before things get crazy," she whispered, with all fight gone.

"Angel," he said, stepping closer, and his heart shattered as she backed away from him.

"Why you running from me like I'ma put my hands on you? You know that's not even in my character," Saleem said, his voice raw with emotions.

"If you'll yell at me, who knows what else you'll do. I mean, you've already been lying. Did you even take your vows seriously? Was this all for you to get back at me?" Amira asked, hating that she was showing so much vulnerability.

Frustrated, Saleem ran both hands over his head, ready to yank his hair from the roots. "Look. I don't know what this is or where it came from, but give me a minute to look into it, a'ight? I love your ass with everything in me. There isn't any amount of money that would've made me marry you. That was all me," he said, slapping his chest.

"For your father, though, right? *That* was all for him," she said, sounding as if she dropped a bomb.

She blew all his shit up and didn't care. Amira thought back to her conversation with Youssef in the kitchen that day and shook her head. Men. Fathers and their fucking sons. Of course, this was for the business. Money made the fucking world go round, and Amira felt it spin right now. It made Saleem bend, betray, and break her heart.

"No." Saleem sighed. "I told you that. Let me call

him and see if he knows where this came from. This has to be fake."

"The irony." Amira scoffed, grabbing the handle of her suitcase.

While Saleem called his dad, Amira took that as her chance to leave. She hadn't packed much and honestly didn't want to pack a thing, but she needed at least the bare necessities. She hadn't called anyone or hadn't fully processed what was happening.

She'd come home and was excited to check the mail. With her last name legally changed, she had to update everything. The main thing she was concerned about was her insurance. She had great benefits, but Saleem's were better. Amira was confused when an envelope addressed to them both fell from the stack. Thinking it may have been a wedding card or something from one of his family members, she opened it. Like Saleem, she couldn't read past the first few lines without tossing it.

Now, she was ready to be done with it all. She loved him... would probably love him until the hate settled in. Blinking back tears, she strolled past him. The rollers of her suitcase sent Saleem into a panic.

"Amira," he said calmly, and his dad picked up the phone.

She ignored him.

"Pops, what is this?" Saleem shouted, walking behind her. "Amira! You're not leaving me!"

She kept on walking.

"Hello?" Youssef said. "What's going on?"

Reaching out for her, Saleem quickly thought better of it and grabbed the handle of the suitcase instead. With ease, he removed it from her grasp. Amira whipped around with fury in her eyes.

"You can let me leave! You've done it before!" she shouted with trembling lips.

Saleem threw her suitcase damn near across the room. "And I'm not doing it again," he said, so eerily calm Amira was afraid to see what happened next.

"Saleem!" Youssef yelled.

"Baby, just give me a minute, a'ight? I got my dad on the—"

"Non."

The one word he told her she could say to him under certain conditions was mumbled so lowly, but it carried the weight of the world and knocked Saleem's breath out. They stared one another down, eyes mimicked with tears, shattered hearts matching, too. They really were twins.

"I'm on my way over there," Youssef said, snapping Saleem out of it.

"Pops...Pops, man. Look. I need you to explain this shit. She's trying to leave me again over this inheritance I don't know shit about. What did you sign for? I don't know what this is. You gotta tell her this is fake."

Amira wanted to run out the door so she wouldn't further break her own heart by hearing the truth, but she couldn't move. Saleem had his gaze pinned on her so intently, somehow controlling her movements. Her chest heaved as they listened.

"Nothing about your inheritance is fake, Saleem."

Youssef's answer was so clear cut that Amira gagged and tossed a hand over her mouth while Saleem's knees buckled.

"How? What do you mean? I didn't agree to this shit!" he spat.

"You didn't have to agree. Your inheritance was contingent upon my approval of seeing you happy," Youssef said.

His words made Amira grip the edge of the entry table. *What does he mean?* Her mind ran down the conversation she and Saleem had that day in his office when she asked about getting married.

"Will your parents be upset? Your dad specifically?" Amira asked.

Saleem shook his head. "Nah. I mean, my mama and sisters might be pissed. My dad is chill. He just wants to see me happy."

"Oh. I make you happy?" Amira asked cautiously.

Saleem hadn't stopped grinning and showing his pretty ass teeth since she came back into his life.

"Very. I'd be even happier if you gave me a kiss," he said, smirking.

Gasping, Amira covered her mouth for a different reason this time. Saleem truly didn't know anything about his inheritance, and Youssef further proved that he wasn't lying.

"I needed you to show me that what y'all had was real. *You* needed to believe that what you and Amira had was worth giving a second chance without the notion of money being the end goal. You needed to learn what it truly means to have a partner... a wife. I needed you to feel and see what it's like to provide, protect, love, and care for your wife."

Amira was so shocked by his words that she felt numb. Wholly and utterly gutted of all feelings. She didn't think she could cry anymore until Youssef continued, and Saleem wiped his face.

"You didn't have to prove anything to me but prove to yourself that you are a man and can fulfill this role in Amira's life. I saw how you all's breakup changed you. It broke your heart. It made you believe you weren't good enough, and that wasn't the truth. She broke up with you for *her*... and saved you in the process. It had nothing to do with you."

Saleem blew out a sharp breath and finally felt the feeling return to his body. He, too, had been gutted thinking that this was their ending again. He took cautious steps toward Amira, and he couldn't mask his shock when she met him halfway. Pulling her into his chest, Saleem hugged her so damn tight that her back popped.

"You there?" Youssef asked.

Saleem cleared his throat. "Yes. We're here."

"Good. That's how it's supposed to be. I didn't tell you anything about the inheritance because it wasn't your business. I don't care how old you get. I'm your father and will always want the best for you. Amira is your best."

She rubbed his back with her face buried into his chest until Youssef called her name.

"And Amira?"

"Yes," she mumbled.

"I want to apologize for making this an issue in your home. Those were never my intentions."

She didn't have a response and was thankful Youssef didn't expect her to.

"You're going to have to fight in marriage. Not physically, but to stay grounded and trust that the foundation you built was meant to last. So, yeah..." He sighed, ready to let them go. "That was my wedding gift to you all. Even though I should've kept it since I wasn't invited."

Amira and Saleem smiled for the first time in what seemed like forever. That dark cloud once hanging over them vanished, and everything around them seemed to come back to life.

"Aye... Pops man." Saleem huffed. "You owe me a fade. Do you know what I just went through over here?"

Youssef chuckled. "I can imagine but tell me what happened when I see y'all on Saturday. My wife is cooking, and y'all better not disappoint her by staying at home trying to make up. Go spend some of that money."

Amira chuckled. "We'll be there."

He smiled on the other end. "I can't wait to see you, daughter. Love y'all."

Youssef hung up, and Amira stayed wrapped around Saleem. The way she just showed her ass had her so embarrassed, but her feelings were valid.

"Angel," Saleem said, and she shuddered.

"Hmm?"

Saleem lifted her head.

"I'm *so* sorry for yelling at you. You gotta know that."

Amira thought to tease him and joke about how his heart was pounding in his chest but didn't. This was the time to be serious because his love for her was nothing to play with, and she knew it.

"I know. We were... pissed at each other," she said gently.

"Yeah, but still. I'll never raise my voice at you again."

She nodded. "Okay. I'm sorry for hollering at you, too."

"And what else?"

Her brows dipped. "What else what?"

"What else you sorry for? My heart is still a little broken by you thinking I was going to hit you. That's..." Saleem shook his head, unable to finish his sentence.

Amira kissed his beard chin three times, still wrapped in his arms. "Natural reflexes. I'm sorry for that, too."

"I can't believe he did all that so I could prove a point to myself." Saleem chuckled.

"Right. You gotta give it to him, though. That was

the true definition of love. Can't nobody tell Youssef about his son," she teased, and they chuckled.

Swiping some hair out of her face, Saleem licked his lips. "You know who nobody can tell me anything about?"

Grinning, Amira shook her head. "Nope. Who?"

Pressing his lips against hers, Saleem squeezed her tight and confirmed with unwavering certainty, *"My wife."*

EPILOGUE
"SHE GON' BE MY WIFE. I TOLD HER THIS ALREADY."

EPILOGUE

Months Later

"I bet you cried again, huh?" Najee asked.

Saleem smirked, holding the phone to his ear while looking out at all his family and friends.

"You'd shed a tear too if you had what I had, bro," Saleem said earnestly.

Najee blew out a breath, clutching the jail phone in his hand. He hated being locked down, but his moment of freedom was approaching.

"Nah. I feel that, man. Renae ass playing and don't want a nigga to put a ring on it."

He chuckled but Saleem didn't. Telling him that his girlfriend of five years wasn't the one he should be tying down would do nothing but stress him out. Saleem couldn't have his boy in that cage going crazy like that.

"You know what you gotta do when you get out then," Saleem hinted, a smirk appearing seeing the men in his family shower Amira with money.

She looked surprised and genuinely happy as money floated around her and pooled at her feet. Since they had already gotten married, they decided to throw a small celebration. It couldn't even really be considered small with the guestlist of one hundred and four people all in attendance, but that was fine. The more, the merrier.

"Yeah...I gotta few things lined up when I get home," Najee said, his words sounding contemplative.

"Saleem!" one of his little cousins yelled, running up to him.

Seeing her mouth full of silver teeth, hair decorated with confetti, and pretty chocolate face covered in cake made him chuckle.

"Slow down, Bia. What's up, pretty girl?"

She blushed. "Amira is looking for you."

"Okay. Tell her I'll be right there."

"Okay! Hurry up!" Bia took off running again, and he shook his head.

Saleem watched as they began gathering all the bills scattered about. Amira was giggling with Jazmine, Quinn, and his sister Yuhani. When she lifted a one-hundred-dollar bill and handed it to Quinn, he couldn't help but wonder what that was about. Amira had to pay up, and she did.

The jail commotion on his phone took him back to Najee's reality. "G?"

"Yeah, bro. Go ahead and enjoy your wife and family. I'm proud of you. I can't see your face, but I can hear it in your voice... that love shit sounds good on you. Prolly got you glowing and shit."

Saleem chuckled. He wasn't lying. "I 'preciate that. Keep yo' head up in there and stay out the way," he said.

"Always."

The call disconnected, and Saleem headed back inside the ballroom of the venue Youssef owned. As soon as Saleem crossed the threshold, the DJ put on one of his favorite album's intros, and he cracked a grin while searching for Amira. He knew she was behind this and had sent Bia to get him.

Coulda sworn that you told me, Bryson Tiller sang, and Saleem bobbed his head, grinning

Amira strutted to meet him in the middle of the floor with the tail end of her dress clutched in her hands. Whoops and hollers echoed around them as they sang the song to one another.

Pointing at her, Saleem sang lowly. "I'm telling you. Nah, I ain't through. I ain't through. I ain't done with you," Saleem's deep voice crooned, making Amira blush like always.

"Sing it, baby," she encouraged, and he got into performance mode. He spread his arms and hit a smooth jig to the beat.

"Okay, brother!" Tayah yelled, recording them on her camera.

Amira matched his energy. "I said with Mira, it's different."

"Let Saleem show you the difference."

They chopped and screwed the lyrics and continued singing. When the beat dropped, and the song transitioned into *Let Em' Know*, the entire dance floor sang along. Meaning the lyrics with everything in him, Saleem rapped them in Amira's face. The way these two songs described their union was so uncanny. Ducking his head, Saleem kissed her lips, and his hand instinctively rubbed her belly.

"You and baby girl good?" he asked in her ear.

Amira nodded. "Yes. I just ate some cake, so she's going crazy."

Moving his hand around her belly to feel her, Amira helped him out and guided his palm to her right side. At twenty-three weeks, baby girl was in her womb having a blast. Saleem smirked when he felt her kick, and his heart swelled.

"Don't eat no more. She wildin'."

Amira cackled. "Please go away. Your mama made me a pan of peach cobbler."

"A whole pan, Angel?"

"Mhm. Should I share it with you?"

Saleem licked his lips and shook his head. "Nah. You can share something else that's sweet, though. Let's go find a room right quick."

Amira backed away from him, laughing and shaking her finger. "I can tell you no now."

"My baby is the condition. Wait until she gets here," he said, smirking, and then the music lowered.

Their attention went to the stage where Jazmine stood with the mic in her hand. She asked for everyone to take a seat at their assigned tables. The crowd dispersed, and with a hand on her back, Saleem guided Amira to theirs. It was in the front, but off to the side because she didn't want to feel too overwhelmed. Once everyone got settled down, Jazmine began talking.

"Hey, everyone," Jazmine said sweetly.

The crowd replied with an array of greetings.

"So, as you all know, I'm Amira's best friend and baby girl's god mommy," she said, waving at Amira, who was grinning.

If people didn't know, Jazmine would let it be known who she was and what Amira meant to her.

"Girl, we know!" Tayah yelled.

"It's okay, Tay. I'll let you see her once a month," Jazmine teased and continued. "The reason I'm up here is obviously to congratulate Saleem and Amira on their union."

The family and friends went wild celebrating them. Saleem had his arm draped around Amira as she leaned into him. She did a cute wave, making a few folks chuckle.

"Yes, yes. Give it up for them," Jazmine said, then focused on the couple. "So, I found a video of y'all from college."

Amira's eyes widened with curiosity. "A video? Babe, what video?" she asked Saleem, who shrugged.

"I don't know. We about to find out, though."

"I came across it looking through my college stuff

and knew I had to show y'all," Jazmine explained. "Is it okay to play it for everyone?"

"It better not be anything crazy!" Amira shouted.

"Crazy good," Jazmine said and blew her a kiss. "Dim the lights, please."

The lights lowered, and a calmness washed over the room. The large projector was fuzzy for a few seconds, and then it cleared, bringing the young couple into view. A boyishly handsome twenty-two-year-old Saleem rocked a fuzzy pony-tail, a black Southern State shirt, though he didn't go there, and a pair of basketball shorts low on his waist.

Beside him, Amira had her hair all over her head, springing with curls popping every which way, and her newly budding loc stood out. She wore Saleem's Nike sweatshirt and cotton gym shorts, showing off her long legs. They'd just left her dorm to grab a bite to eat and weren't prepared to get stopped by anyone. Especially not someone wanting to interview them.

Definitely not after what they'd just been doing. Saleem could still taste her on his lips and smell her all over him. He hoped ol' girl wasn't trying to chat for long.

"Hi! My name is Mel. I'm one of the writers for

our school's newspaper, Onyx Press. Do you guys mind if I interview you for next month's issue?"

Saleem looked at Amira, and she shrugged. "Yes, that's fine."

"Perfect. Let me adjust my camera really quick," she said, going behind the camera that was screwed onto a tripod. She pressed a few buttons and walked back to them. "It'll just be a few questions, and I'll be out your faces."

"And the video?" Saleem asked, tossing an arm over Amira's shoulder, pulling her closer to him as students walked by.

Their pose then was similar to how they were seated now. Up under each other... in one another's skin.

"Oh. We have a website where we try to post things. Heavy on the word try," she said and chuckled. "Not every video gets uploaded, though, so no worries. I'm not going to sell it or anything."

Amira smiled and hid her face in Saleem's chest when he whispered, "She could've sold the one we just made."

"Hush," she hissed and straightened when Mel appeared ready, holding a notepad and blue pen.

"Okay. What's your names, and what year are you in?"

He waited for Amira to go first, but she nudged him to go ahead. "My name's Saleem. I'ma senior at RSU."

Mel focused on Amira, and before she could say anything, Saleem answered for her. "This is Angel."

Amira playfully rolled her eyes and smirked. "My name is not Angel. That's just what he calls me."

Mel smiled so big when Saleem kissed Amira's cheek.

"My real name is Amira. I'm a freshman, and I go here," she answered.

"What is one thing you guys want in life once you graduate?"

Saleem answered first. "I graduate this year, and the only thing I want is some rest."

They all chuckled. Senior year was no joke, but he'd be good once graduate school began. Everyone had been telling him that the workload was lighter.

"Nah. For real...I want to build a legacy for my family," Saleem added.

"And what about you?" Mel questioned Amira.

She shrugged a little. "Um...I'm not really sure. I guess happiness. Even when things are going bad in the world, there's a little bright side somewhere in something that brings joy."

"Yes, there is. I love that answer."

She paused and read over her notes. "Now, I know this is far out and probably not even on your mind right now, but do you guys see yourself still being together years from now?"

"Ummm," Amira began but didn't finish, thanks to Saleem answering.

"Yeah. She gon' be my wife. I told her this already," he said coolly.

Amira looked up at him with tiny stars in her eyes, wondering if he could see the future. She hadn't been thinking that far ahead but found it cute that he was.

Everyone in the crowd made an *awww* sound. Seeing them this young and in love, so sure and kind of hesitant about what they had, was a full-circle moment.

When Saleem looked beside him at the table, Amira was giving him that same look from years ago. The one that could get her anything she wanted. Only the stars now were brighter and bigger, filled with sureness. Her eyes glossed a bit as she thought back to her answer in Professor Ross' lecture hall that day.

Fate...

Back then, Amira didn't believe in its certainty.

She ended things with Saleem out of fear. Fear of their potential and the unknown. She let the opinions of outsiders sway her decisions when they didn't know her...didn't know them. They damn sure didn't know him.

She walked away with insecurities clouding her journey when she should've let their love unfold naturally.

Now, Amira moved with love at the forefront of her heart. The kind of love she and Saleem had always shared and now created life with. He had always been an unwavering constant she could rely on no matter how complicated her emotions became.

That hadn't changed and never would. Together, they were building a life they were meant to have. Fear of what would come next no longer existed, and whatever it was, they were ready for it.

Maybe Saleem could see the future after all.

BONUS SCENES

BONUS SCENES

"Look at you," Amira cooed, rubbing both hands over her belly.

At seven months pregnant, baby girl had made her presence known and was running things already. The snug fit of her orange two-piece workout set from Curve Me was almost comical. Her belly stretched the leggings to their capacity while the fitted tank top had officially graduated to a crop top. She tugged at the hem like it would magically grow.

Smirking, she said, "You done made me have to get a whole new wardrobe. It's okay, though, mommy's baby."

Amira had gotten lucky during the first five or so months of her pregnancy, being able to wear clothes already in her closet. However, that all seemed to change overnight. Now, she had a section and pile of clothing that was too uncomfortable to even consider squeezing into. Huffing, which was all she did nowadays no matter the task, she brushed her hair into a low ponytail, leaving out her bedazzled loc.

Done in the bathroom, she walked inside her closet. Eyeing the shelves of shoes, she grabbed the most comfortable pair. Putting them on her feet was a full-blown obstacle she wasn't in the mood for today. So, she headed out of the closet and out of their bedroom to find Saleem. They were supposed to be going for their mid-day walk, and she knew he was patiently waiting for her. Like he always had been.

Saleem must've felt her coming to find him. His smooth, deep voice greeted her before she could enter the kitchen. "You good, Mama?"

Amira couldn't help but blush as she waddled to him. Her nicknames now alternated between Angel, Mama, and her favorite one, *My Wife*. Hearing him claim her with so much love and affection in his voice made her giddy and emotional. He was a proud husband and father-to-be, and let it be known.

When she made it to him, Amira was so caught up in his bare chest and the gray sweatpants hanging low on his waist that she quickly forgot what they were supposed to be doing. She had other plans in mind that would surely make her out of breath.

"Mmhmm," she hummed, poking her lips out for a kiss.

Bowing his head, Saleem kissed her lips and grinned when she rubbed her hands up his chest. He rubbed her back while she wrapped her arms around his neck. For a moment, they stayed like this. Eyes closed, body to body, basking in the simplicity of it all. Their lives had changed so much in less than a year, and while they should've been overwhelmed, they were at peace. The kind of peace that only comes when you're loved and in good hands with the person meant for you.

When Amira pulled away after sniffing his neck like an addict and massaging his scalp, she had tears in her eyes. Playfully, Saleem poked his lip out.

"What's the matter, baby?" He asked.

Amira shrugged. "I don't know. I'm just happy. And you smell good. And I can't put my shoes on."

The tears fell, and she swiped them away. Saleem helped her, using the pad of his thumb.

"It's okay to be happy. If you weren't I'm not doing my job. You want me to put your shoes on for you?"

She nodded, chest heaving as she breathed hard. "Yes. This baby has me so emotional. I'm sorry."

"You apologizing for no reason. Cut it out," he softly fussed, then kissed her again. "Cry all you want to. I have something that will cheer you up."

Her eyes lit up, and Saleem smirked, already knowing what she was on.

"Some dick?" Amira asked. Her eyes dropped to his waist, and she tugged at the band of his sweats.

"Nah." Saleem laughed. "Is that the only thing I provide that makes you happy?"

Amira smirked. "I meeean, no. But it's a damn good incentive to cheer me up."

"You be crying on this mothafucka, too, so I don't know how," he joked, making her roll her eyes.

"Whatever."

The irony of a man offering her the same thing months ago held no weight to her man, her husband, giving her some dick right now. Amira would happily take all of him.

Saleem was and had always been in a league of his own. He'd give her whatever she wanted, but right now, sex wasn't it. Walking toward the refrigerator, he opened it and pulled out a mason jar filled with bright yellow juice.

"I made you a new mixture. I think you'll like this one," Saleem said.

He grabbed a gold-rimmed glass from the cabinet and popped the seal on the jar before filling her glass. Leaning against the island, Saleem watched her sip slowly and grinned when her eyes widened. A sure sign that whatever concoction he'd come up with was more than just good. Before she could give her praises, Amira guzzled the juice down.

"It's hitting, huh?" he asked.

Amira licked her lips. "Yes. What all did you use?"

"I can't tell you. It's a secret," he teased.

"There's pineapple in it, I know that."

Saleem nodded. "Yeah. What else did you taste? Did you even taste it? You drank it so fast." He laughed.

"I don't know why you're acting like I'm not eating, drinking, sleeping, and doing everything else for two. I was thirsty."

"I'm playing with you, Angel. Here," Saleem said,

reaching for her glass. He refilled it and handed it back to her.

"See. How hard was it to do what your wife wanted you to do in the first place?" She asked, smirking.

"*My wife* gon' get her ass bent over this counter if she keeps looking at me like that," Saleem said. His voice lowered to that octave that made Amira lose all train of that.

Instead of responding, she lifted the glass to her lips, smirking behind it. In the end, she always got what she wanted anyway.

"Thank you for this. It's really good," she said.

"You're welcome. That's not really what I had for you, though. Come in the living room."

Amira watched the muscles in his back flex as he twisted the lid back on the jar and placed it inside the fridge.

"I thought we were going walking?" Amira asked

"We are."

"Do you see my body in this outfit? I can hardly fit my workout clothes anymore." She pouted, and Saleem shook his head.

Walking toward her, he lovingly rubbed her belly before kissing the top of it. "Your body is cold, baby. You're still fine as hell, just carrying an extra blessing now."

Amira rolled her eyes but couldn't fight the warmth spreading in her chest or her cheeks as she grinned. "You're just talking."

"Speaking all facts." His copper eyes dipped to hers, softening in a way that always turned her heart and brain to mush. "We can go shopping after our walk."

Amira gave him a look. "You mean after our nap?"

Saleem's laugh was deep and low, making her nipples hard from the sound alone. Everything or nothing at all aroused her these days.

"I gotta take a nap with you?" He asked, humored, already knowing what she was going to say.

"Yes. So you can rub me to sleep. Now, come on so you can show me what you got me."

Saleem smirked. "You got it, Mama. Come on."

His hand protectively found the small of her back as they walked to the living room. Saleem didn't rush her; just walked at her pace. He made sure she was comfortably seated when they got to the couch.

"You're making me nervous," Amira said, chuckling.

"I am?" Saleem teased, knowing exactly how her nerves were set up.

Amira didn't respond. She just watched him reach behind the loveseat on the other side of the room and pull out a sleek black box with gold lettering and a red bow on top. Squinting, trying to figure out what it was, she accepted it when he handed it to her.

"You got me a gift?" She asked.

Saleem nodded. "A lil' something I know you wouldn't have gotten yourself."

"But...I didn't get you anything. If I'd known we were exchanging gifts a month before Christmas, I would've had you one, too."

She was whining, and that shit made Saleem feel a tad bit bad, but not entirely. What he did for her didn't need to be reciprocated in the same manner. Saleem didn't want her to feel pressured by a gesture he knew would make her smile. That was enough for him.

"You and my baby girl are the gift, Angel. Stop whining and see what you got," Saleem said.

The pout never left her face since he told her so eloquently. Amira stared at the box, her hands trembling slightly. Not expecting anything but always receiving something from Saleem should've been nothing new. He was a listener and a provider. A man who had, from day one, put in the work to see Amira happy. He wasn't going to stop now that she was his wife or carrying their daughter. Saleem only had plans to go harder for them both.

"Can you at least sit down? Hovering over me like that," she mumbled, and he smirked.

Hormones kicking her ass, he thought, sitting down beside her.

Amira eyed him before flipping the latch on the box. Her eyes widened as she pushed back to the top. This was one gift she never expected him to get her, but it let Amira know that he *really* did listen to her. The box held a complete tattoo kit for beginners. A shiny machine, a power supply system, bottles of ink, practice skins, gloves, transfer sheets, and everything she needed to tap into her love for tattoos.

Her jaw dropped, and she looked up at him. "Babe... are you serious?"

He leaned forward, arms resting on his thighs. "Dead serious. You were talking about how many more tattoos you'd have if you learned to do your own, so… now you can. Isn't this a side hustle you mentioned in college?"

She nodded with watery eyes. "Yes, but… that was so long ago. How do you even remember that?"

"Nothing about you is easy to forget."

Amira blinked, her emotions bubbling over. She set the box beside her, then turned to him. Hugging him around the neck, she squeezed tight and kissed his lips. "Thank you so much, baby. You didn't have to do this."

Saleem shrugged like it was nothing because it was. "You're my wife, Amira. Whatever you want, it's my job to see that you have it."

Her lips trembled, and she quickly blinked back the tears threatening to spill. "You're too good to me, you know that?"

"Nah," he said, leaning forward to kiss her forehead. "You deserve all this and more."

She sniffled, then laughed, shaking her head. "You better stop before I start ugly crying."

Saleem chuckled. "Ain't like I haven't seen it before."

Amira rolled her eyes, grinning. "Whatever." She grabbed the box again, running her hand over the bottles of ink. "I can't wait until she's here so I can tattoo her name on me."

"I'll do you one better," Saleem said.

Amira raised a brow. "Huh?"

He leaned closer, tapping the side of his neck with his finger. "You can break it in on me."

"You want me to tattoo her name on you?"

"Nah. Your name," he said, turning his head to expose the left side of his neck. "I want it right here."

Amira's eyes widened. "On your neck? You can't be serious."

"As a heart attack," he said, grinning. "Stamp it right here down the side so everyone knows exactly who I belong to. I'm all yours, baby."

She stared at him, her mouth hanging open. "Saleem, I've never done this before. What if I mess up? I can't have you out here looking like someone scribbled on you like a desk in ISS."

Students with bad behavior had in-school suspension and would be so bored just drawing on anything. Amira wasn't trying to have him out here bad like that.

He chuckled and shrugged like it didn't faze him. "Then I'll be rockin' a messed-up '*Amira*' on my neck, and I'll still wear it proudly. You got me or what?"

Her laugh was shaky as she started pulling

things out of the kit. "You're crazy. You know that, right?"

"Crazy about you," he said, kissing her temple, watching her excitement take over. "You know I love you, right?"

Amira nodded. "Yes."

"As long as you know that. I'ma go grab you a table tray."

He stood up and was about to walk off, but Amira grabbed his hand.

"I love you, too," she said softly but firmly.

Saleem gave her a wink that lit her face up with a smile. Simple, cute shit like this was what she loved the most. When he returned with the tray and a chair for him to sit in, she began unpacking everything, focusing on every tool. She'd always wanted to become a tattoo artist just for fun but hadn't gotten around to pursuing the hobby.

Once she was ready, Saleem settled in his seat, tilting his head to the right. Amira stared at him, wondering how he was so comfortable with this.

"Are you nervous?" she asked.

Saleem glanced at her. "Nah. It's you. Why would I be?" The trust in his eyes and the casual way he gave her the green light to ink his skin made her chest tighten. His confidence in her settled her nerves a bit.

"Never mind," she mumbled, smiling.

After washing her hands, Amira snapped on a pair of gloves then grabbed the practice skin from the kit. She exhaled loudly.

"Okay... let me get a feel for this first," she said.

"Take your time," Saleem told her, leaning back like he had nothing to do.

After a few strokes on the practice pad, Amira straightened up. "Okay, I think I'm ready. You sure about this?"

Saleem tapped the side of his neck, the spot he'd picked out just below his earlobe. "Right here, Angel. Don't make it all small, either. I need people to be able to see that shit without squinting."

Smirking, she swallowed hard, grabbing the machine. "All right. Sit up straight for me."

Saleem adjusted his position, his head tilted slightly to give her better access. She cleaned the area, and the cool swipe of the alcohol pad made his skin glisten. He didn't flinch; he just sat there watching her like she was the most fascinating woman in the world. Grabbing his phone out of his pocket, Saleem opened the camera app, flipped it and started recording.

"My wife about to tat me up real quick," Saleem said into the camera, smiling wide. "Say what's up, baby."

Blushing, Amira waved. "He trusts me so much."

"With my life. You know that."

Amira stared at him, once again, getting off track. Shaking the feeling to straddle his lap, she shook her head. Amira hesitated for a second as the machine buzzed to life, but Saleem's calm voice gave her the push.

"You got this."

That was all she needed. With a deep breath, she pressed the needle to his skin, her hand surprisingly steady as she started outlining the first line of the letter A. The buzz filled the room, providing a sound that made her anxious to keep going.

"How's it feel?" she asked, her voice low, focused.

"A lil' pinch. I'm good," he said, his tone relaxed like he was chilling on the beach instead of getting inked.

Her nerves melted away as she worked, replaced by a strange sense of pride. Each line, each curve, came out cleaner than she'd expected. The red ink looked so good against his skin. Saleem stayed still, his breathing even, letting her take her time. When she finally pulled back to admire her work, she couldn't help the wide grin that spread across her face.

"All done."

Saleem reached for his phone, flipping the camera to check it out. Turning his head, his eyes lit up, and his grin matched hers. "Yo," he said, chuckling in awe. "This shit looks so good, Mama."

A
M
I
R
A

Her cheeks burned, and she smacked his arm playfully. "Don't hype me up too much. It's just my name."

"Exactly," he said, grabbing her hand and pulling

her into his lap. "Your name on me, forever. That's a flex."

Amira looked at the tattoo, and her heart swelled with gratitude. "I got your name on me, too," she said, wiggling her wedding ring. "Thank you for trusting me. I'm so happy now."

Saleem kissed her cheek, his hand resting on her belly. "Good. That's all I ever want to make you."

Amira realized it was more than a tattoo when she looked at her name again. It was proof of their bond and his commitment to her, not just by marriage but in everything Saleem did. He was no longer worried about the what-ifs and never had a thought about what he'd cover her name with if they were no longer together.

Their bond was unshakable, unbreakable, meant to be, and written in ink. Amira was about to go crazy with her new toy, and Saleem had a few spaces for her to practice on and add his baby girl's name when she arrived.

Their bedroom was quiet except for the tranquil sounds from the small water fountain on their dresser. Amira loved the one in Saleem's office so much that he bought a few to place around the house. Amira sat curled up in the reclining chair, her head resting on a pillow, nursing a mug of *Blow* tea. Across from her in the bed, Saleem lay shirtless, cradling their three-week-old daughter against his chest.

Sahima Destiny Majid was the perfect mixture of both of her parents. She entered the world with a head full of curly black tendrils, curious penny-colored eyes like her daddy's, and everything else mimicking Amira's features. Dressed in only a diaper, Sahima's tiny body rose and fell with Saleem's steady breaths. His large hand supported her back, holding her tiny frame like she was the most fragile, precious thing in his world.

"You sure she's comfortable?" Saleem asked, his voice low and careful.

Amira smiled. Her eyes were heavy from lack of sleep but filled with love. "She's fine, babe. Skin-to-skin is good for her. And you."

Saleem looked down at Sahima, his heart swelling at how small she was. Her soft, caramel-colored skin pressed against his, and her little fingers curled into tiny fists as she squirmed slightly. She settled quickly, her cheek resting on his chest, her breaths syncing with his.

"Man, she's so tiny," he murmured, his fingers gently brushing over the sparse curls on her head. His deep voice seemed to soothe her, and the little furrow in her brow disappeared as she nestled closer. "I can't believe we made her."

Amira chuckled softly, pulling the blanket up around her legs. "Believe it, Daddy. That's all you right there, stealing hearts already."

Saleem glanced her way. "You must want me to put another baby in you, calling me that."

Amira blushed, hiding behind her mug. "I mean... at least wait a few months. Goodness."

He licked his lips and smiled. "I'll wait as long as you need, Angel. She looks like you, though. Look at her little nose and her lips. She's your twin."

Saleem was in love. He cried when she came out wailing and wouldn't let anyone except Amira hold her for the first hour she was born. Sahima had no idea how spoiled her daddy was about to have her. Standing up, Amira placed her mug on the nightstand and slowly climbed into bed beside them.

"She's gonna have your feet," Amira teased, rubbing her sock-covered foot.

Saleem laughed quietly, careful not to disturb their daughter. "Good. She can keep her foot on folks' necks."

Amira rolled her eyes but couldn't help grinning. She watched as Saleem shifted, adjusting on the pillow and letting Sahima stretch out against him. His hand spanned nearly the entire length of her back, holding her securely. Amira couldn't stop her eyes from watering.

"She loves you already," Amira said softly, her voice tinged with awe.

Saleem's eyes never left Sahima's face as he spoke. "She's my whole world. Both of y'all are." His voice cracked slightly, and he cleared his throat. His hand rubbed softly over her tiny back. "I didn't think I'd be given the chance to love anyone like this."

Amira blinked back tears. She was thinking the same thing.

"You're a natural, you know that?"

"Nah," Saleem said, his voice barely above a whisper as he kissed the top of Sahima's head. He inhaled her scent, and it calmed his racing heart some. "Nothing natural about this. I'm just learning as she grows. I'm learning with you, too. I'm just taking my time with all of this. For you and her."

Sahima let out a soft coo, and her tiny body completely relaxed against his. Saleem smiled, and his hand stroked her back in gentle circles.

"See how she's already trusting me to hold her down? I can't mess this up."

Amira leaned over, running a hand through his scruffy beard, and massaged it. "You won't."

Saleem met her eyes. They were so vulnerable, and Amira knew being a father had brought out so many different emotions in him.

"I look at her and look at you and..." he stopped and shook his head. "Everything makes sense. All we went through. The doubt, the years apart, the miscommunication for a bit. None of that matters. She was made out of love, and I can't get over her being made with you. My Angel."

Amira sniffled, wiping her face. Of course, he'd make the tears fall. "We're so lucky to have you."

"Nah," Saleem said, his voice was thick with emotion. "I'm the blessed one. Thank you for giving us a second chance."

Amira kissed his lips and mumbled, "You gave me no choice, really. I was always going to be your wife, remember?"

Saleem smiled, and Sahima let out another small sigh. "I'm glad you know." Looking down at their daughter, he kissed her forehead again. "Sleep tight, princess. Daddy got you and Mommy forever."

He wouldn't call it luck... especially when they were always meant to be. Whatever it was classified, someone, somewhere, had been looking out for them both, and for that, Saleem was beyond grateful. He'd gotten the family he always wanted, and Amira got her happily ever after plus more.

The End

DISCUSSION QUESTIONS

Should Amira have broken up with Saleem?

Should Amira have accepted his offer?

Was Saleem wrong for not telling Amira about Brandi?

Would you have done what Amira did after Saleem hadn't explained the situation?

Do you feel Saleem pursued Amira for his own reasons, or was it true love?

Do you think Youssef should've told Saleem about the inheritance?

Who's story do you think is next?

AUTHOR NOTE

I hope you enjoyed Amira & Saleem's book just as much as I loved writing it. I **did not** want to share Saleem at all. When his character first came to me in April, I knew he'd be something special. Then, the snippet of him in Here With You Forever set the tone for the kind of man he is. The type of man he was for Amira.

My signature style of writing my male characters is always, "Who does this man need to be not only for himself but for the female main character as well." Does his morals and character align with the story and the overall plot? It's not always about creating a book bae, and that's never my goal. I want you, the reader, to always feel like the MMC fulfilled their role in the books, whether you liked him or not.

I have to give it up to my girl Amira. She didn't play about her boundaries. Even though she was young and made some decisions she regretted, she stood by them. Just because you have a history with someone, mother or not, it doesn't mean you have to go against your morals to make someone else comfortable. What did Jazmine tell Amira? Let it flow or let it go. If someone no longer aligns with who you're growing to be, cut them off. Continuously pouring from a half-full cup to fill someone else's cup isn't fair to you. Pour more into you in 2025 and cherish the relationships that do the same.

This book mentions a few characters from my back catalog. If you want to read about them, their books are listed below.

Lucci & Enzo - She From The Gutta
Synovi - Keep You To Myself

ACKNOWLEDGMENTS

ACKNOWLEDGMENTS

All praise to the Man above for blessing me with a gift and allowing me to share it with the world. I'm forever grateful!

Thank you to every reader who supports me! If you enjoyed the book, please be sure to leave a review when you can and tell a reader friend about it.

To my cover reveal and ARC team, you don't know how much I appreciate you! Thank you for going above and beyond for me.

I hope y'all are ready for 2025!